Henry Sinclair
and the Dream Riders

Henry Sinclair
and the Dream Riders

The Destiny Chronicles

ADAM S. CROWE

RESOURCE *Publications* · Eugene, Oregon

Resource Publications
An Imprint of Wipf and Stock Publishers
199 W. 8th Ave., Suite 3
Eugene, OR 97401

www.wipfandstock.com

PAPERBACK ISBN: 979-8-3852-3663-3
HARDCOVER ISBN: 979-8-3852-3664-0
EBOOK ISBN: 979-8-3852-3665-7

02/25/25

All rights and ownership of the following images were generated by the
author under Midjourney and Adobe terms of service.

To Cooper, thank you for letting me tap into the depths of your imagination to bring this story to life . . .

To Emmie, Max, and Ty, thank you for being the first to be introduced to Henry and letting him come off the page . . .

And lastly . . . to Jennie and Liam, thank you for listening to every "great" story idea I had over the years and allowing me the time and space to distill those thoughts into the adventure that follows.

Contents

PROLOGUE

The Un-Laboratory

THE SPACE WAS NOT really a laboratory in the traditional sense. Laboratories were brightly lit areas with clean and organized work surfaces that would be used to develop the next great innovation, technology, or "thing" (as kids like to say).

Tools, equipment, and materials were scattered across several workbenches, in addition to assorted snow globes, newspaper clippings, and other assorted knick-knacks that lined the work areas like a crowd of expectant onlookers.

The persistent gasoline smell, occasional visit of a small mouse (affectionately named Timmy), low lighting, and overall dingy feel felt like the opposite of a laboratory. An un-laboratory, if you will pardon the parlance. Considering it was a small garage space, an un-laboratory is about as good as it would get.

A tall, lanky man with long hair stood nearly shoulder-to-shoulder with a shorter, dark-haired woman in front of one of the workspaces. She held orange, yellow, and blue wires in place while the taller man soldered it to a green-colored square plate covered with various wires, cables, coils, and resistors.

"I think that's the last adjustment," The tall man said, removing his protective glasses. "We shouldn't experience any additional issues during our next transit."

The woman took the square plate and slid it into one of the arms of a pair of dark-colored, bulky, oversized sunglasses.

"I still think we should have tried to make a time machine," the woman said with a smile.

"What would we make it out of—a train?" The man said as he adjusted his gold-rimmed glasses.

"You always did like trains." The woman said dismissively.

"Did I ever tell you I was a train conductor?" the man asked.

The woman smirked. "Yes, you did. You were a train conductor at an amusement park."

"That counts!" the man called out.

Their shared laughter was drowned out by the loud squeak of the garage door rolling open.

A second man stepped into the tight confines and rolled the garage door back down. He turned to face the tall man and the dark-haired woman. In the low lighting of the space, the shape and shadows of this new man's new face were long and sharp as if a knife had been pulled from the shadows into existence.

"I did it," the knife-faced man said. "I found the final pieces."

"Where did you find the parts?" the woman asked. "Was it for that secret government defense project?"

"Yes," the knife-faced man said dismissively as he moved over to the work benches. "I built them a weapon of used pinball machine parts and took the real parts we needed."

"That seems unethical, Xander," the tall man said.

"I don't remember asking you," Xander replied.

Xander pulled a small package from his pocket and laid it on the nearest workbench. He opened the top flap and revealed three small cylinders neatly tucked into a bed of loose packing material. Even in the low light, the three cylinders glowed red, yellow, and blue.

"I call it a sleutel," Xander said with a mischievous grin. "It means key."

"Will they control the chaos?" The tall man asked.

Xander reached into the box and handed the blue cylinder to the man and the yellow cylinder to the woman. He kept the red cylinder which seemed to make his already sharp, knife-like facial features glow red.

"Three keys to start the dream matrix," Xander said.

" . . . and three keys to stop it, right?" The woman asked.

"Of course," Xander said with a wave of his hand.

The room was quiet around them as if anxiously awaiting their next decision.

"Will they work?" The woman asked nervously.

"There's only one way to find out," Xander said with a smile.

Xander, the tall man, and the woman each picked up a pair of the oversized sunglasses they had been adjusting earlier. Even in the low lighting of the room, the lenses of each pair were dark enough that they seemed to be pulling all surrounding light into them like a visual vacuum.

All three placed the glasses on their faces and plunged their visions into total darkness. The darkness was like falling into a well leaving behind the cramped quarters of their small un-laboratory.

Within a few seconds, the tall man, the woman, and Xander disappeared, leaving the oversized glasses clattering to the floor.

40 Years Later . . .

1

Clement and the Cat

IN A SMALL WHITE house on the south side of Maclin Avenue, an older man sat at a small green Formica table in the corner of his living room. The table had originally been labeled avocado green when he bought it many decades prior, but now it was worn down and dulled by age. Even the silver edging of the table was marked with rust and years of patina. The table leaned slightly to the side much like the man did.

Instrumental music filled the room from a record player set at the end of a nearby table. The black round vinyl record spun at a steady speed under the small needle. The man gently swayed to the soothing rhythm.

Puzzle pieces of various sizes and shapes were scattered across the table before him. The lid of the puzzle box sat propped against a large book so the man could see the picture on the front. A small horse was taking shape inside the mostly finished rectangle of edge pieces. The man's tufts of thinning, wispy white hair waved from the slight breeze blowing in from the nearby open window. He stretched his arms back and groaned slightly as the bones and muscles of his back strained against gravity and age.

The man adjusted his gold wire-rimmed glasses which rested at the very edge of his long, elongated nose. Only after years of practice had the man mastered the ability to perch them at such a precarious angle.

A cinnamon-colored house cat curled up on top of a nearby leather ottoman. He licked his paws, stood, and returned to the comfort of her coiled peace.

"Where is that puzzle piece, Copernicus?" The man said to the cat. "You didn't eat it did you?"

The man smiled at his joke.

Upon hearing his name, the cat jumped down and slowly meandered toward the puzzle table. He wrapped his body around the table leg before hopping into the man's lap (as was their regular practice) to receive a vigorous rub behind the ears.

"It's a horse running through a field, Copernicus," the man said. "Think you can keep an eye out for any missing pieces?"

As if satisfied with the attention (but likely simply exercising fickle cat discretion), Copernicus jumped back down from the man's lap. He quickly ran to the open window and jumped up on the sill looking out into the street.

"Time to watch the birds, eh?"

The cat ignored his question and continued to look out the window.

The man secured another puzzle piece, finishing the horse's head and connecting it to a meandering river behind the image of the horse. He picked up another piece but dropped it quickly as his cat let out a loud hiss.

"Do you hear something, Copernicus?"

The cat ignored the man and remained focused on his view of the yard and street in front of the man's house.

The man stood and walked over to the record player. He quickly snatched the needle up creating a loud scratching sound and breaking the tranquility of the room.

The man tilted his head to the side and pinched his eyes closed as he focused on the sound.

The cat hissed again as car doors slammed outside the man's house.

As fast as his legs would move him, the man moved to the window and pulled back the curtains to look out the same direction as his cat.

The color quickly drained from the man's face. As his arms dropped, the curtains ripped from the wall and fell in a puddle around his feet. The cat meowed in disapproval.

"Oh my gosh," the man said. "They found me. I don't know how, but they found me. Run for it, Copernicus."

The cat followed the direction without hesitation, jumped from the window sill, and scurried toward a nearby house.

The man shuffled across the room toward a black rotary-dial phone that sat haphazardly on two old phone books near the now-silent record player. He picked up the handset and began spinning the yellowing numbered dial in a quick and confident order. Once he was done dialing he pressed the handset to his ear and waited.

Ring.

Ring.

Ring.

A voice picked up on the other end.

"Leigh? Is that you?" The man said. "It's me, Clement."

Clement listened to the response.

"I know," he replied. "I'm not sure how they found me, but they did."

Clement listened to the voice and nodded several times.

His focus was interrupted by three loud bangs on his front door.

"They're here!" Clement yelled.

Three more loud bangs echoed through the room.

"We know you're in there!" A voice shouted from the other side of the door. "Give us what we want and we won't hurt you."

Clement's already pallid face seemed to sink in on itself. He licked his lips and blinked several times.

"Listen to me, Leigh," Clement said to the caller. "I'm going back in there. You'll know where to find me. We can't let him get all three keys or he'll shut it down forever."

Clement slammed the phone's handset back into the cradle causing the internal bell to ring. He sat in the nearby leather chair causing a poof of dust to erupt around him. A small wooden figure of a mallard duck sat on the nearby table. Clement reached over and turned the mallard in a full circle. A trap door opened in the side of the table revealing a hidden compartment.

Two more bangs at the door. Clement could see his old wooden front door was beginning to break. Panels of wood in the door were now splintering.

Clement removed an oversized pair of darkened glasses from the hidden compartment on the side of the table. They were attached to several long wires.

Three large men dressed in all black burst through Clement's front door. A tall, lanky man walked in behind them. His piercing blue eyes focused immediately on Clement sitting in the chair.

"Ah, Clement," the tall, lanky man said. "It's good to see you again."

Clement's lips were tightly pinched and his eyes were narrowed as he shook his head.

"I see the pleasure is all mine," the tall, lanky man said. "In that case—give me what I came for."

"You can't have the key," Clement spat at him. "I'll never give it to you."

"Oh, Clement, you don't have to give it to me," The man said, knocking over the puzzle table. "I'll just take it."

A sly smile curled onto Clement's face. "Xander, you'll never find me or the key again."

Clement threw the glasses onto his face and leaned back into the chair. With a flash of light and a loud pop, Clement was gone.

2

Grandma's Kitchen

FAR FROM CLEMENT AND his cat, Copernicus, was the small town of Miller's Landing which was named after famed (or perhaps infamous) explorer and adventurer David Miller. It sat on the edge of the Aileron mountains not far from Patriot's Hollow. On the far west side of town, Waldroup Avenue ran for several blocks and was lined with older but well-cared-for homes.

At this time of the afternoon, Waldroup Avenue was quiet as schools had not yet let out for the day. The normal raucous noise of kids at play and the soft whirring of cars returning from work commutes was absent.

A small white postal delivery van was running its route down Waldroup Avenue. Jimbo Johnson—the local mail carrier—had run this route for the previous ten years. He slowly and methodically added envelopes, parcels, and other mailers into each mailbox, in turn. The truck's brakes squealed slightly as he stopped at the next house. He made a quick mental note that he would probably have to get that fixed soon.

This house had a regular, unremarkable black mailbox. Underneath the box, a small wooden name plate swung in the soft afternoon breeze. It simply said, "Shipp."

"Hey, Jimbo," a woman said from the side of the house. "How are you today?"

"I'm fine, Mrs. Shipp," Jimbo replied.

"Jimbo, please." The woman replied. "Call me Leigh."

The woman wore a red and black plaid shirt over rough-hewn work pants tucked into tall green rubber boots. Wisps of silvery-white hair fell from beneath the brim of her oversized straw hat.

"Working the garden today?" Jimbo asked.

"You guessed it," Leigh replied with a smile. "My grandkids are coming over later today so I wanted to see if anything in my garden was ready to pull."

"Any luck?"

"Not really," Leigh said as she absently pushed the loose hair back from her face. "The birds and squirrels seemed to enjoy the garden more than I have."

The birds and squirrels had definitely taken their share, but Leigh had never really had much of a green thumb. She had enjoyed spending time gardening with her husband, but it had been many years since he was able to help her.

Jimbo nodded and handed Leigh a small stack of mail. They exchanged one more round of pleasantries before Jimbo pulled away to finish his delivery route. Leigh knocked the dirt off her boots and walked back inside her house.

She put her hat on the top peg of the coat rack and set her boots at the bottom. Leigh's house was neat and tidy as it had always been. She took personal pride in her ability to "keep a good house" as her mother had often said. With her grandkids coming she was not sure how long the house would stay this way, but she would have it ready nonetheless. For the next hour, Leigh put out fresh sheets and linens, filled the candy jar, dusted counters, and swept the floor.

By mid-afternoon, Leigh glanced at her watch and realized that her family would be here within the next hour. It was the perfect time to start making her world-famous (at least in her own opinion) peanut butter cookies. She loved the smell of freshly baked cookies. Her husband had too.

She moved into the kitchen and adorned her favorite apron (which read "there's no place like home—except grandma's house") which her grandkids gave her for her birthday last year. She pulled out the flour, eggs, sugar, and peanut butter (homemade from a neighbor down the street). She also pulled out a bag of those little chocolate-covered peanut butter cups which Leigh felt were the secret ingredient. She folded the ingredients together, placed them in rough circles on the baking sheet, and slid them into the oven she had preheated.

She moved to the sink and began to wash the mixing bowl, measuring cups, and spoons that she had used. After the cleaning, cooking, and cleaning again, Leigh hoped sleep would come easily tonight. She glanced out the kitchen window hoping to see the arrival of her daughter's gray station wagon filled with her wonderful grandchildren.

Leigh's phone rang. She turned off the water in the sink and dried her hands on her apron. She moved toward the faded creme-colored phone attached to the wall.

"Hello?" Leigh said as she moved back to the window, still hopeful of the arrival of her family.

"Leigh?" The voice asked. "Is that you?"

"Yes," She replied with a frown. "Who is this?"

"It's me, Clement."

"Clement?" Leigh whispered. "We agreed not to make contact to ensure it was protected."

"I know," the man replied curtly. "I'm not sure how they found me, but they did."

Leigh absently stroked a small cylindrical object hanging from a long string around her neck.

"You need to get out of there right now," Leigh demanded. "They can't find your part. He'll destroy it for everyone."

Leigh could hear loud banging in the background and now heard the sound of a car pulling up in front of her house. She glanced out the window but felt her stomach drop. Instead of her daughter's gray station wagon, there was a long, black SUV parked in front of her house. The windows were tinted such that she could not see who was inside.

"They are here!" Clement said.

"They are here too." Leigh sighed.

"Listen to me, Leigh," Clement said. "I'm going back in there. You'll know where to find me. We can't let him get all three keys or he'll shut it down forever."

Leigh heard a click as the phone call was disconnected. She could hear car doors opening and closing outside. She quickly pulled the sheet of cookies from the oven and slid them onto the counter, tipping over the container of sugar and knocking the butter dish to the floor.

There was now banging on her front door.

Leigh quickly moved to the living room at the back of her house. She slid along a narrow bench in front of a small wooden organ. She put her left hand across the keys, resting them gently across the ivory. She inhaled deeply before beginning to play. Upon the clink of the fifth note, a mechanical click and loud swoosh emanated from a hidden door to the side of the organ.

As the door opened fully, it revealed a small room lit by only a few blue lights. A large, cube-shaped table sat in the center of the room. Leigh walked into the room and flicked a switch, causing the door to slowly close. With the hidden door nearly closed (and hidden once again), she glanced back just as the front door of her house blew open shooting splinters across the room.

3

To Grandmother's House We Go

BECKY SINCLAIR'S LONG, BONY fingers gripped the steering wheel tightly and she maneuvered her well-loved station wagon through rush hour traffic. She had not allocated the extra twenty minutes needed for the full-blast, five-alarm fit her teenage daughter had thrown about leaving to visit her grandmother.

Tiffany—the daughter in question—had claimed she had never been told about the trip, but Becky was nearly certain she had told her last week at breakfast. Admittedly, until Becky had finished a full cup of coffee in the morning (from her favorite cup reading the erroneous—"Happy Birtday"), she lacked the mental clarity to confidently recall what she had told her daughter. The last thing she remembered was instructing Tiffany to drive her son, Henry, and his best friend, Dickie Dubois, to the store to shop. Something about needing a new shirt? She could not recall.

"Thanks for letting Dickie come along," A dark-haired boy said from the back seat of Becky's station wagon. "He'll be way better company than Tiffany."

"Henry, don't say that about your sister," Becky said, glancing in the rearview mirror. "But you're welcome nonetheless."

With a huge smile on his face, Dickie sat in the seat next to Henry looking out the window as the traffic jam finally began to clear.

Although you could not tell from their sitting position, Henry was nearly a head taller than Dickie which was unremarkable to these two best friends. Outside of the height difference and opposing hair colors (Dickie's head was filled with blond-colored curls), they were a true dynamic duo. It warmed Becky's heart that her one and only son had such a strong friendship at this age.

"Thanks again for letting me come, Mrs. Sinclair," Dickie said.

"You're welcome," Becky replied with a smile as she changed lanes to maneuver around a slower-moving truck.

Dickie would be a much easier travel companion than Tiffany would have been. Before leaving her behind, Tiffany indicated that taking her on the road would literally, figuratively, and possibly even spiritually wreck her life. Her plans (loosely described as "hanging with her friends") could not be interrupted. Tiffany even implied that her grandmother was so old she probably would not even notice her absence.

"Do you think Grandma will mind that Dickie is with us?" Henry asked.

Becky took a deep breath. Henry's question was reasonable, but far too complicated to answer easily.

"Mom?" Henry asked. "Did you hear me?"

"Yes—of course," She replied. "Grandma will be fine with Dickie being here. She'll be disappointed that Tiffany isn't coming, but she'll understand that Tiffany's a teenager and therefore often acts like a teenager."

"Teenagers," Dickie said with forced authority. "Am I right?"

Becky smiled at the sentiment. With Henry and Dickie only two years away from their teen years, she had her doubts that they would be any different.

"That's not to say that she may not seem sad," Becky added.

"Because of Grandpa?" Henry asked quietly as his smile faded slightly. "Because of his sickness?"

Becky locked eyes with Henry in the rearview mirror and nodded.

"What's wrong with your grandfather?" Dickie whispered to Henry.

"Something with his brain," Henry said, leaning closer to his friend. "Like he gets details all mixed up and can't remember stuff sometimes."

"Oh, geez," Dickie said with a wave of his hand. "My Pop-Pop does the same thing. He can't remember where he put his keys or his coffee mug all the time."

"It's not like that," Henry said dismissively. "He gets really confused about where he is and who we are."

Henry paused and looked out the window as the trees whooshed by.

"My mom says he even acts out sometimes—mean like a devil," Henry continued. "Nothing like he used to be."

Dickie nodded and became quiet.

"He's been sick most of my life," Henry said quietly.

Dickie stared out the window as Henry began reading the most recent Fabulous Five comic book, whose cover showed a furious battle of tendrils and tentacles between Commodore Goodman and Webmaster against Evil Emily and Mandussa. As always when reading about his favorite superhero team, Henry was able to quickly escape into a dream-like world filled with the battles of good versus evil and leaving thoughts of his sick grandfather behind.

Becky continued her drive from Patriot's Hollow zoning out to the sounds of contemporary adult music (which Henry thought was terrible) and the consistent rumblings of the highway headed north toward Miller's Landing.

"How much longer 'til we get to Grandma's?" Henry asked his mother.

"We've got about ten minutes," she said as she placed a piece of trail mix into her mouth. "I bet she'll have some fresh-baked cookies ready for you guys."

Dickie's eyes widened as big as saucers at the possibility of fresh-baked cookies awaiting his arrival.

"I wonder what flavor they will be?" Dickie asked greedily. "Peanut butter is my favorite."

"I'm a sugar cookie fan, myself," Henry said, leaning back in his seat.

He could almost smell his grandmother's cookies. His mother was right that his grandmother typically baked cookies for their arrival. Henry could often smell the delicious aroma on the front porch stoop far before he made it into the house. That same smell was magnified inside and washed over them like waves on an ocean of deliciousness. Henry was not sure he could have dreamed up a better experience.

Becky smiled at their enthusiasm. "I'm sure they will be scrumptious no matter what the flavor."

Henry quickly tucked his comic book away and began to watch the horizon eager to see signs they were getting closer.

"What is your grandmother's house like?" Dickie asked. "Other than the cookies I mean."

Henry pondered his friend's question. He could have described the color of the walls (mostly maple-colored wood paneling) or the texture of the aged shag carpet, but that did not seem to be what Dickie was asking. He could have told him about the number of bedrooms or the cluttered office where his grandfather used to conduct his accounting business. Henry was definitely not going to share that. They had talked enough about his grandfather already.

"What do you want to know?" Henry asked.

"Like when you close your eyes or have one of those crazy dreams where you visit your grandmother's house—what do you see?" Dickie suggested.

Henry closed his eyes and took several deep breaths thinking about his grandmother's house. As ideas flashed through his mind, he felt an overwhelming sense of love, but then the answer became clear.

"Snow globes," Henry said as he opened his eyes.

"Say what?" Dickie asked, wrinkling his nose.

"You know—snow globes," Henry said with a smile. "She's got what seems like hundreds of those little plastic globes with buildings or roads inside that you flip over, shake, and it snows."

"I think my Mom has one of those from her trip to Smith Lake," Dickie nodded at the description. "Seems kind of weird to me because it snows at Smith Lake like once every hundred years."

Henry and Dickie both laughed.

"We are almost there, boys," Becky said from the front seat.

Henry sat up straighter and glanced over his mother's shoulder. The scenery had changed significantly. He no longer saw empty farm fields and a sea of trees. This was decidedly more domestic. The street was filled with similar-looking houses evenly spaced and lined up in straight lines.

Becky slowed her car and turned into the empty driveway of Henry's grandmother's house. Henry and Dickie quickly unbuckled and jumped out of the vehicle. Becky stepped out too and stretched her arms high over her head.

The three of them walked down the sidewalk toward the front door.

"It looks like your grandmother left the door open for us," Dickie said as he pointed to the open front door.

Henry glanced at the open door, but it did not look right. There were several places where he could see large wood splinters like the door was damaged. He glanced at his mother and could see her face looked concerned.

"Grandma?" Henry shouted as they approached the door. "Are you there?"

Becky stepped inside the now damaged door and looked around. Henry and Dickie stepped up next to her and did the same. The house was a mess.

"Something terrible has happened here," Becky said quietly. "Boys, call the police."

4

Broken Snow Globes

THE TALL, LANKY POLICE officer pulled his utility belt up with both hands causing the cuffs, flashlight, keys, and firearm to rattle in a disorganized orchestra of clicks and clanks. The belt (and its various dangling weights) seemed to defy gravity particularly, on the officer's thin frame. He pulled out a small notepad and pen to take notes as he listened to Henry's mother talk.

"So you discovered that the door had been forced open?" The police officer asked Becky. "And the lock was broken?"

"Yes, that's correct," She replied curtly.

"Was there anything valuable taken?" The officer asked, looking around the room. "Like electronics, jewelry, or money?"

Henry followed his gaze across the flipped tables and tossed chairs. Pictures that were previously hanging neat and straight on the walls were now tilted haphazardly or knocked to the floor entirely. In the kitchen, sugar was spilled across the counter and sticks of butter were scattered across the floor. A tray of peanut butter cookies sat on top of the stove. Dickie picked up one, inhaled, and sat it back on the tray with a look of utter disappointment.

"I have no idea," she replied quickly. "We called you immediately once we arrived."

The police officer nodded as he pulled up on his utility belt again.

"We're gonna need to know that," he said to Becky.

Becky ran her hands through her hair and inhaled deeply before locking eyes with Henry.

"Can you look around?" Becky asked Henry. "Maybe take Dickie and see if you see anything that has been taken?"

Henry grabbed Dickie by the elbow and led him further into his grandmother's house leaving his mother to continue her conversation with the heavy-belted police officer.

"What exactly are we looking for?" Dickie whispered.

"I'm not sure," Henry said. "Let's just see if anything looks weird."

"Like this?" Dickie said, picking up a green book from the floor.

Henry looked at the book (a first edition of *Mushrooms, Toadstools, and Regional Fungi*) and shook his head.

Henry was not sure what they would be looking for. He knew what his grandmother's house was like, but the details were fuzzy. He had never once thought about anything of value in her house. He had no idea about her jewelry, money, or other precious items. As for electronics, his grandmother had one television set that had a wooden box with gold inlay around it as if it was imitating a fine piece of furniture. Under that television, a large flat video gaming console was stored with its two knobbed joysticks peering above a layer of dust like beacons of a not-so-modern age. Henry had once played a game on it with his grandmother where a large white square-shaped ball bounced back and forth between the players to his grandmother's utter delight.

The television and video console seemed untouched.

Henry led Dickie down the hallway past several bedrooms that seemed mostly untouched. He stopped at the hall bathroom and flipped on the wall switch. The soft glow of the fluorescent lights made the mauve tiling less inviting than Henry remembered. The only thing out of place was a small wooden plaque that had fallen from the wall. Henry picked it up and wiped it with the back of his hand.

It was a picture of a green landscape with a quiet river cutting through the land. Henry frowned.

"What's that?" Dickie asked as Henry hung the picture back on the wall.

"It's my grandmother's favorite picture," Henry replied quietly.

Dickie watched his friend and put a comforting hand on his shoulder.

"I'm just worried about her, Dickie," Henry said.

Henry and Dickie walked to the back of the house into a long rectangular living room. A small wooden organ sat against the wall on the near side of the room. A long, olive-green upholstered couch lined the wall opposite a large panel of windows. A picture of a vase of lilies hung over a small end table that held one small, red glass candy jar filled to the brim.

"Hey look," Dickie said pointing to a table in front of the window. "Is this what you were talking about in the car?"

Henry glanced in the direction Dickie was pointing. The remnants of dozens of snow globes were scattered across the top of a long wooden table under the windows. Refracted rainbows of color spread out across pools of water as the broken domes of glass redirected the light from the window. The glass glittered and winked at Henry seemingly oblivious to the harm that had been inflicted.

"It looks like they broke every one of them," Dickie whispered. "Why would they do that?"

Henry shook his head. He felt his chest tighten in worry. These snow globes meant everything to his grandmother. With them lying scattered and broken across the table, all he could envision was his grandmother hurt by the same people who had broken the snow globes.

"It's almost like they were looking for something," Dickie said absently. "Like how bad guys would search for a secret key or something."

Henry ignored Dickie's suggestion and walked over to the organ stool and sat down.

"What in the world happened here, Dickie?" Henry asked. "Who would want to break into an old lady's house, break things, but not take anything of value? I couldn't even dream this up."

"Me neither," Dickie said, leaning against the wall next to the organ.

Henry laid his hands gently on the keys. He could see both of his grandparents sitting in this very spot playing a variety of songs. The green cover of *Spencer's Organ Player Songbook* sat closed on the music sheet holder.

Henry closed his eyes tightly as if he could hear the hum and tinkle of the organ being played by his grandparents. Instead, all he could hear was the worried tone of his mother's voice in the other room as she continued to discuss the break-in with the officer.

Henry opened his eyes and opened the songbook. He turned near the middle and pushed the sides flat on the holder. Henry stood tall on the stool and posed his fingers above the keys ready to perform.

"What are you going to play?" Dickie asked, still leaning against the wall.

"It's a song called *Lilies of the Deep*," Henry said. "It was my grandmother's favorite song. She taught it to me when I was younger."

The fingers of Henry's right hand quickly pinged three notes between white and black keys followed slowly by two notes with his left. Instead of the continued notes of his grandmother's favorite song, there was a loud click followed by a soft hiss. Dickie fell through a newly opened gap in the wall he had been standing against.

"Ouch," Dickie said, rubbing his hip where he had fallen.

Henry quickly slid from the organ bench and landed at Dickie's feet. He could see his friend's legs lying on the well-aged green shag carpet. But Dickie's head, arms, and torso were lying on hard black stone that was illuminated by low-level, recessed blue lights.

Dickie sat up and looked around at tables and counters covered in various tools, equipment, and technology that looked straight out of the future.

"Holy cow!" Dickie yelled. "It looks like your grandma built a secret room."

5

The Secret Room

HENRY REACHED DOWN AND helped Dickie back up to his feet. He stood in the newly opened doorway and looked back and forth. Henry could still see his grandmother's house with her old couch, worn carpet, and broken snow globes on one side, but the other side of the doorway was a whole new world. This new space was cold and dark. Heavy black benches wrapped around the edge of the room which reminded Henry of the science lab at his school. Henry could not have dreamed of such a place.

"You okay?" Henry asked Dickie as he looked him over.

"Oh sure," Dickie replied, knocking dirt from his hands and looking around the room. "Just shocked is all."

"I know what you mean," Henry whispered.

Henry had no idea what this room was or why it was there. He had been to his grandmother's house dozens of times before and had sat at that very organ and nothing like this had ever happened.

"Why is there a secret hidden room in the back of my grandmother's house?" Henry asked.

"It's like a superhero lair or secret lab or something," Dickie said.

Henry nodded. The secret room had the vibe of superhero headquarters, right out of one of his Fabulous Five comic books.

"Maybe we should tell the cop—or at least your Mom—about what we found?" Dickie asked.

Henry glanced around the room again and felt torn. He was still worried about his grandmother (and what may have happened to her), but this room was straight from the coolest dream he had ever had. He also had a nagging feeling that this room might be the key to unraveling what happened to his grandmother.

"Let's not tell them," Henry said, walking toward one of the benches.

Dickie raised his eyebrows in surprise.

" . . . yet," Henry said, sheepishly.

In front of Henry was a black workbench covered in various tools and parts. A large roll of blue wire was rolled up to the side on top of a large stack of yellowed paper. Coils of different sizes, shapes, and levels of rust sat next to the wire and paper. Henry picked up a pair of yellow-handled pliers and squeezed them experimentally.

"Do you think your grandmother built things here?" Dickie asked.

Henry shrugged.

"My grandfather liked to think of himself as a carpenter," Henry responded. "Maybe this was his workshop?"

"Pretty low light for cutting wood," Dickie scoffed. "That's a pretty good way to become Three-Finger Sinclair."

Henry turned around and faced the rest of the room. In the low light, he could see a large square box in the middle of the room. It had no tools, equipment, or papers on it like the benches around the walls did. The bench was a deep black color which seemed like it was absorbing what little light was available in the room. Henry felt there was something peculiar about this bench. It was out of place in a room that was out of place. Henry walked toward it, drawn like an insect to a blackened flame.

"Speaking of lights," Henry said, "let's see if we can find a switch."

Dickie walked toward the benches and began running his hands over the darkened surfaces trying to find the elusive switch.

"Nothing here," Dickie said over his shoulder.

Henry nodded. He walked straight for the dark black box and slowly ran his hands along its mysterious surface. The box was cold to the touch—much colder than the surrounding room conditions. It was also incredibly smooth under Henry's probing fingers.

"Find anything over there?" Dickie said with an edge of disappointment.

Henry rolled his finger over the side and down along the first edge finding nothing more than continued cold. He dropped to his knees and felt along the side closest to the door, but still found only smooth lines of the cold box.

"There's gotta be something here," Henry said from his knees. "Keep looking."

Henry slid around to the side of the cube opposite Dickie. Given the low lighting of the room, this side was the darkest of the four. He placed his hands together near the top and began to slide them slowly side to side, back and forth. Henry could sense the taste of disappointment settling into his gut. He had hoped this room was the key to figuring out what happened to his grandmother. He closed his eyes and let his hands roam free then he stopped and his breath caught in his chest. Henry could feel the raised edge of a button sitting under the fingers of his right hand. It was warmer and rougher than the surrounding surfaces of the black box.

"I think I found something," Henry said as he pushed the button.

A hum immediately filled the space. Henry could feel a vibration emanating from the box. A loud click triggered and then a bright blue light illuminated the edges of the top of the box. Henry glanced across the top of the box and locked eyes with Dickie whose eyes were as big as saucers and whose mouth was agape.

Henry stood up and put his hands on the edge of the box directly across from Dickie. Four rectangular-shaped holes had opened in the top of the black box. As if lifted from beneath a theater stage, four pairs of dark-colored glasses rose in their place. As Henry picked up the glasses, he realized they were not like regular glasses. Dark lenses were wrapped in black frames and arms that felt like the same material as the box. They were also much heavier than Henry had expected. When he looked up, Henry realized that Dickie had been looking at the pair of glasses in front of him as well.

"These are the strangest sunglasses I've ever seen," Dickie said. "Like who needs sunglasses in a room this dark?"

Henry glanced out the secret door and could still see his grandmother's living room. It stood frozen in time just as he remembered it, but the secret room stood in stark contrast.

"Let's try them on and see how we look," Dickie said with a smile.

Henry nodded and unfolded his glasses but kept them in his hands.

"Can't hurt anything, right?" Henry said quietly. "Let's do it."

Henry slid the glasses up on his face. They fit surprisingly well on his nose and ears and felt much lighter on his face than in his hands.

"How do I look?" Henry asked.

"I don't know it's so –," Dickie said.

But before he could complete his thought, an image formed in front of them on the black table.

"Do you see this?" Henry said.

A large floating egg shape formed in front of the two boys and was slowly spinning. Long tendrils were growing from the top and wrapping down each side. The other side was starting to have a texture with two matching dips and one larger bump appearing in the middle.

"Yeah," Dickie said excitedly. "It looks like a person."

The egg was shaped into a face with more details and textures appearing. The tendrils were now clearly hair and the shapes Henry had seen were eyes and a nose. A pair of glasses now appeared over the developing face and numerous lines were appearing, giving it a wrinkled look.

"It's a face," Henry gasped.

The rotating face stopped in front of Henry and blinked twice. Henry realized he had been holding his breath and exhaled deeply.

Quietly, the secret door closed, shutting off both boys from the outside world.

"Hello, Henry," the face said. "It's Grandma."

6

The Scientist

"GRANDMA?!" HENRY YELLED.

"Well, yes," the floating head said. "And no."

Henry blinked twice. His brain felt foggy. He had the sensation of being in a dream. His missing grandmother's face was floating and talking to him in a secret room at the back of her house. This felt real and looked real but could not be.

"This is your grandmother?" Dickie asked, stepping back from the table, but not removing the glasses.

"Yes. No. I don't know," Henry said frustratedly.

The floating head was smiling now.

"You're probably wondering what is going on," his grandmother's head said. "I'm sure this is all very confusing."

"You can say that again," Henry replied to the floating head. "What are you? Who are you?"

"Henry, listen to me," Grandma's floating head said. "I don't have much time to explain."

Henry nodded, still unsure what he was looking at.

"Technically, I am a computer-based augmented reality program," the floating head said. "I used to call it CARP, but that didn't work well. It sounded too much like an ugly fish."

"So you're just a computer?" Dickie asked.

"I'm much more than a computer," the floating head responded. "Your grandmother recorded a message for you earlier today
which is put into this form by C.A.R.P. so you can interact with me."

"So we can ask you questions?" Henry said eagerly.

"That's correct."

"Where are you?" Henry asked quickly. "Why is your house
all messed up? Who broke into your house?"

The floating head seemed to ponder Henry's string of questions to decide which to answer.

"My apologies," the floating head said slowly. "I am having
difficulty processing your questions."

Henry leaned back frustrated at the interaction.

"Perhaps you could ask a different question?" The floating
head asked.

Henry closed his eyes tightly causing lines in his forehead to
appear pinched together as if the right answer could be squeezed
out.

"What should we ask now?" Dickie asked.

"New question," Henry said. "Can you please play the message recorded by my grandmother earlier today?"

The floating head smiled and nodded slightly.

"Yes," the floating head said. "Give me a moment to process."

Henry and Dickie both watched as the eyes of the floating head flickered and blinked several times before returning to the steady appearance it previously had.

"Hi, Henry," the floating head started. "If you are finding this, I was right to believe that if anyone would find it you would. There isn't much time so I will try to make this brief. Unfortunately, a dangerous man named Xander Dirwyn sent men to my home today. They weren't able to hurt me—or find me—but I imagine my house is in shambles."

"That's an understatement," Dickie mumbled.

"Why was this man—Xander Dirwyn—trying to hurt you?" Henry asked, frowning.

"You're probably asking yourself, 'Why would Xander Dirwyn try to hurt me?'" The recording continued. "Years ago—long before I met your grandfather—I worked in a laboratory as a scientist. I had two partners—Xander Dirwyn and another man named Clement Crowne. Xander, Clement, and I did research in neurobiology and neuromolecular divergency. In essence, we studied the mind and all its intricacy."

"Your grandmother was a scientist?" Dickie asked in disbelief.

"A brain scientist, I guess," Henry said flatly. "I thought she was just good at baking cookies."

"One day," the floating head continued. "Xander, Clement, and I made the most amazing breakthrough—we called it dream riding."

"Did she say dream riding?" Dickie asked, confused.

"We found a way to access everyone's dream," the floating version of his grandmother's face said. "We found a way to visualize and access the dream space of every single person on the planet."

"Like real dreams?" Henry asked. "Not like some sort of time machine?"

"A time machine," Dickie echoed. "Now that would have been cool."

The CARP machine paused, flickered, and glitched again.

"No, it's not a time machine," the floating head said. "Would you like me to continue with the recording?"

"Yes, please," Henry said quickly.

"Xander, Clement, and I spent many years exploring the dreamscape—that's what we called it," she continued. "We had numerous breakthroughs in our understanding of how people's dreams reflect their physical, mental, and spiritual well-being."

Henry's face flushed at the thought that his grandmother would have seen his dream last night of six clowns riding surfboards while singing nursery rhymes in three-part harmony.

"Unfortunately, over time the three of us began to splinter," the floating head continued. "Clement and I agreed that the dreamscape should be protected, but Xander began to think it could be controlled, manipulated, or even sold."

Henry realized he was gripping the CARP table tightly and nervously wiped his sweaty hands on his faded jeans.

"To protect the dreamscape, Clement and I made certain sacrifices and agreed to move on with our lives in isolation to prevent Xander from causing harm."

"Sacrifices?" Dickie asked. "What kind of sacrifices?"

The CARP box continued seemingly ignoring Dickie's question.

"Unfortunately, Xander found both of us," she continued. "Clement called me and let me know that he was planning to flee into the dreamscape. When Xander's men arrived at my house too I saw no other option. I, too, fled."

" . . . into the . . . dreamscape?" Henry gasped. "What does that even mean?"

The CARP unit froze and flickered for a moment before responding.

"My apologies," the floating head said. "That completes the rest of the message."

"Is my grandmother okay?" Henry asked desperately.

"I am unable to provide a clear answer," the floating head said dispassionately.

Henry pulled off the glasses and threw them onto the black box where the CARP system had been running. Dickie took his off and walked toward his friend.

"I can't believe your grandma invented a . . . dream machine," Dickie said.

"You believe all that?" Henry asked quickly. "That sounds like the craziest thing I've ever heard."

Henry's head was spinning. He had previously just been worried, but now he was confused and conflicted. The vision he had always had of his grandmother had been destroyed. He had never thought of her before as anything more than a cookie-making, game-playing, loving woman he called Grandma. He had a feeling of disbelief. The idea of dream riding was impossible. He felt a growing sense of irritation, but he was not sure why. If true, Henry was upset that his grandmother had hidden this part of her life for so long. If this was all some big ruse, why would his grandmother go to the effort?

"What do you want to do?" Dickie said, interrupting Henry's thoughts.

"What do you mean?" Henry asked.

"Should we tell your Mom?" Dickie said slowly. "Like tell her about the room, the message from your grandmother, and the whole dream riding thing?"

Henry snorted. Dickie's question was reasonable but sounded so outlandish to Henry's worried ears.

"I don't think we can tell my Mom until we figure out what is going on here."

"But we know what's going on?" Dickie said. "Your grandmother's message explained it all."

Henry closed his eyes, rubbed his face, and ran his hand through his hair.

"Let's call her bluff," Henry said as he pointed to the glasses sitting atop the black box.

"Do what?" Dickie asked.

Henry walked back to the black box, picked up the glasses again, and quickly pushed them back on his face. Dickie followed him and did the same thing.

From inside the lens, the floating head was still visible spinning slowly in a circle.

"Please access the dream riding interface," Henry said.

"What are you doing?" Dickie whispered.

Henry ignored his best friend's question as the CARP unit froze and flickered like before.

"The dream rider interface is loading," the floating head said coolly.

Instead of the floating head, Henry and Dickie now saw a three-panel display. To the left was a spinning globe shape with a line running through it that wiggled slightly from side to side. To Henry it was similar to how a compass looked. To the right, a panel held a series of numbers and letters under a header that read "Destination History." The middle panel had six spinning wheels that reminded Henry of a locker combination. The words "Target Destination" hovered above the combination. Beneath the target destination panel was a large glowing red circle that simply said "Go."

"Are you doing what I think you're doing?" Dickie exclaimed. "Are you trying to go dream riding?"

"You bet we are."

"We?" Dickie said as he swallowed hard.

Henry glanced at the destination history and noted the last number and letter combination. It was a guess, but he assumed this was where his grandmother had traveled. He quickly entered the combination into the center screen.

"You ready?" Henry asked Dickie.

Henry did not wait for an answer.

"Go!"

7

The Station of Dreams

HENRY'S VISION BLURRED INTO long lines to every side as if someone had hooked his belly button and jerked harder than he could
have imagined. Henry instinctively gripped the black table in the
middle of his grandmother's hidden room but could feel his shoes
slipping from the cold dark floor as they lifted upward.

"Henry?!" Dickie called out. "What is happening?"

"I . . . am . . . not . . . sure," Henry yelled as his feet lifted higher
and his fingertips slipped from the box one after another.

Henry reached out and grabbed Dickie's hand just before
his grip on the box failed. The two friends tumbled away from
the hidden room and down a tunnel of speeding lights. Henry's
stomach rolled as the spinning—and lack of discernible floor—left
him confused and disoriented. He closed his eyes and squeezed
Dickie's hand even tighter.

After several deep breaths, the tumbling was slowing and
Henry's disorientation had lessened. He slowly opened his eyes to
see that the stretched light had changed in color. Instead of the
mostly black and white lines, the tunnel of light had transitioned
to a rainbow of vibrant colors like a box of crayons melting across
the table.

"Open up your eyes, Dickie," Henry said. "It's kind of . . . .
beautiful."

While still holding hands in a vice-like grip, both boys were now looking around as the vibrant colors swirled by. In addition to the color changes, Henry could also smell something warm and sweet. A sensation of comfort washed over him replacing the fear he had initially experienced. He glanced over and noticed a weird, wide grin on his friend's face.

"Where are we going?" Dickie said through his grin. "Do you think we are dreaming?"

"This doesn't feel like a dream to me," Henry said as he shook his head.

"Do you hear that noise?" Dickie asked.

Henry listened closely. Dickie was right. There was a faint noise that was different from anything they had heard before. It was a repetitive noise that felt as much as sounded like a throbbing sound.

"It's like a thump, thump, thump," Dickie said.

Henry nodded.

In addition to the thumping sound, Henry could now hear something else. It was a higher-pitched sound, almost like a whistle.

"I hear something else now, too," Henry said concentrating. "It almost sounds like my sister when she used to try and play the flute."

The fear was building for Henry. He could feel it tickling the back of his mind. His mouth was dry and he was having trouble breathing.

Dickie coughed several times to his side.

"You okay?" Henry asked.

"Not sure," Dickie said, coughing again. "The color seems to be fading."

Panic was rising again for Henry. Dickie was right that the color of the tunnel was no longer as vibrant as it had been earlier.

Dickie coughed harder this time.

Henry's eyes were watering and his throat felt scratchy, too. Henry realized that the tunnel was filled with smoke.

"Quick!" Henry yelled. "Cover your mouth."

The boys both covered their noses and mouths with their shirts. Henry swished his hand side to side in a futile effort to wave away some of the smoke just like his mother did when she burned something on the stove.

The thumping and whistling noises were getting louder as the smoke filled the area around them.

"It almost sounds like a train!" Dickie yelled over the noise.

"A train?" Henry coughed against the smoke. "Why would there be a train here?"

"I think it's clearing," Dickie said.

The tunnel which had started black and white and moved to a rainbow of colors now seemed to be evaporating altogether. Natural light seemed to be seeping in from all directions and the smoke was dissipating.

To Henry's wonder, he looked down to the realization that both he and Dickie were sitting on a seat in a train car. He quickly glanced the other way and saw a long line of windows shining light from every angle. Henry and Dickie quickly ran to the window.

Henry could see the front of a neon train curving around tracks up ahead. The engine's brightly colored smokestack billowed bright pink smoke that curled up into the sky. The smoke was puffy and light like cotton candy at a community festival. The train's wheels were also unusual. Not only were they large—much taller than Henry and Dickie—they looked inflated like a pool inner tube.

The engine was brightly colored with a large painting on the side. Henry thought it looked like a mermaid conversing with a dragon on top of a large scoop of ice cream (Butter Pecan if anyone is interested).

"Look at that coal car, too," Dickie gasped as he pointed to the car behind the engine.

Where the large stack of black coal should have been stored, Henry could see a pile of the largest chocolate chip cookies he'd ever seen.

"It looks like the tracks end up there," Henry said pointing.

There was a brightly colored red and yellow house adjacent to where the tracks ended. Henry could feel the thump-thump of the train begin to slow as it straightened its course and arrived at the station. With a soft hiss and a long, loud whistle the boys jerked slightly in their seats as the train came to a full stop. Henry could see houses and streets all around the station.

"What is this place?" Dickie asked.

"Should we get out and explore?" Henry asked tentatively.

Dickie nodded with a big toothy grin.

The boys walked down the aisle to the front of the car they were in. The doors opened automatically and three steps appeared going down to the ground. Henry went first with Dickie close on his heels. Henry looked up to the front of the house which had a bright pink sign that read:

"WELCOME TO THE STATION OF DREAMS"

8

Marshmallowland

Henry and Dickie stood on the wooden platform of the train station. The whistling and whirring of the train were slowly waning.

"Where are we?" Henry asked as he looked around.

Dickie simply pointed at the Station of Dreams sign that adorned the building next to the train.

Henry rolled his eyes.

"You're suggesting that this is some sort of dreamland?" Henry said.

"Maybe?!" Dickie said with a smile and a shrug.

"Moreover, that my grandmother invented a machine to access this . . . dreamland?" Henry replied.

"That is what she said in the recording," Dickie replied quickly. "How else would you explain it?"

Henry shrugged.

"We just flew through a tunnel of light and appeared in a strange land while riding a brightly colored train that was coughing out pink-colored smoke," Dickie said with a big toothy grin. "I think we're in dreamland."

Henry smiled at his friend, and for the first time since arriving at his grandmother's house, felt joy creeping back into his soul.

"Let's take a look around," Dickie said.

Henry thought the Station of Dreams had an old Western vibe, but the colors were wrong. Everything was painted in crimson red, sky blue, coral pink, emerald green, mustard yellow, and deep violet instead of the expected dusty brown and chalky yellow. Likewise, where horses would have been tied out front there was a string of orange and purple scooters lined up and ready.

"What do you think this means?" Dickie asked, pointing to a small plaque on the far wall.

Henry walked to where Dickie was standing and looked at the plaque which read: "Compliments of CSD Enterprises."

"What is CSD Enterprises?" Dickie asked.

Henry looked at the letters to ponder Dickie's question as the train groaned from behind them.

"Certified . . . Special . . . Dreams?" Dickie asked excitedly.

Henry snapped his fingers and ran his hand through his hair.

"I bet it is Clement, Shipp, and Dirwyn—CSD," Henry said. "Weren't those the names of the other inventors my grandmother mentioned?"

"That's right!" Dickie yelled. "Clement Crowne, Xander Dirwyn, and your grandmother."

"Yep—Leah Shipp," Henry said. "But just Grandma to me."

"Do you think she's here?" Dickie asked quietly.

"She's gotta be," Henry said. "Let's keep looking around and see if we can find anything."

Henry and Dickie walked down to the front of the train station and turned at the corner of the building. The side of the train station was covered in a giant mural. To the left, a white unicorn with a silvery horn stood on its back legs. To the right side of the wall, there was a red and black scorpion with its tail curled back over its body poised to attack the unicorn.

"Looks like a ferocious battle ahead," Dickie said, nodding at the mural. "The tail and horn look equally lethal."

Henry glanced at the wall again and gasped. The scorpion's tail no longer held the dangerous pointed barb, but instead had pincers like a finger and thumb holding a giant horseshoe as if it was ready to play a game with the opposing unicorn's horn.

"Did you see that?" Henry asked dumbfounded. "The picture changed."

Now as Henry and Dickie looked at the picture together it had changed again. The unicorn was now a reindeer with jingling bells hanging along its body and the scorpion had become a giant sleigh filled with brightly wrapped gifts.

The boys continued their walk down the side of the building before coming to an opening near the rear of the Station of Dreams. The land before them opened up widely. Hundreds of dome-like structures sat positioned all over the landscape in every direction. Cobblestone roads ran in every direction cutting in and out of the positioned domes. Up on the hillside far in the distance, a large river was flowing toward the dome structures. It broke into a variety of smaller and smaller streams that split amongst the domes and roadways.

"This place is massive," Henry said. "I guess it would have to be to contain everyone's dreams."

"Let's go inspect one of those domes," Dickie said.

Dickie led Henry down the cobblestone street toward the nearest bubble. Henry stopped on a bridge on the path that crossed one of the streams he had seen earlier. It slowly flowed under the bridge and down the canal toward domes in the distance. It reflected light in a spray of rainbow colors and meandered down the canal in a slow, lazy way that reminded Henry of melting ice cream.

On the other side of the bridge, Henry saw Dickie reading a sign in front of the nearby dome.

"What's it say?" Henry asked Dickie.

"It says "Marshmallowland,"" Dickie answered. "With a name underneath it."

"What's the name?" Henry said, walking toward Dickie.

"It says 'Annabeth Foster, Pascagoula, Mississippi, current age—7," Dickie replied.

Now that Henry was closer he could see more detail in the domes. He could see through the dome, but not clearly. From his vantage point, the inside of the dome was mostly white with flashes of color here and there. It almost looked like a winter snowscape.

The Marshmallowland dome had a hazy quality that shimmered slightly as if it was ready to change its shape at any moment. Henry had the distinct sensation that he was looking into one of his grandmother's old snow globes (before they had been broken).

"I wonder how strong these domes are?" Dickie said. "They don't look very thick."

Dickie walked toward the Marshmallowland dome and gently placed his hands against the dome.

"Oh boy!" Dickie exclaimed. "It's cold and feels soft and squishy like slime."

Henry watched as Dickie's face began to pinch as his grin faded.

"Henry—something is wrong," Dickie said. "I can't pull my hands free."

"What do you mean?" Henry asked quickly as Dickie seemed to plunge his hands further into the dome.

"It's pulling me in, Henry!" Dickie screamed. "I can't stop it. Help me!"

Henry grabbed Dickie around the waist and began to pull, but no matter how hard he pulled Dickie slid further into the dome.

"I'm scared, Henry," Dickie yelled. "What is going on?"

Nearly all of Dickie's body was inside the walls of the dome. His face was turned hard to the side trying to avoid a final plunge into the squishy unknown.

"Don't worry!" Henry yelled, still holding tightly to Dickie's waist. "I won't let you go."

As promised, Henry did not let his friend go. All in one motion, Henry could feel his leverage fail as his feet slipped sending him and Dickie through the edge of the dome and into the sticky unknown.

9

Marshmallows of the Deep

HENRY'S VISION BLURRED FOR a moment and he felt a cold, sticky sensation as he and Dickie fell through the barrier of the dome. They landed together in an awkward embrace, but as they hit the ground they bounced and fell and bounced again before stopping.

"The ground is still wiggling back and forth," Henry said as he looked around. "It's like we are on a trampoline."

"I think I'm blind," Dickie said with a panic as he rubbed his eyes. "All I see is white."

Henry laughed and stood up on the bouncy, uneven ground.

"You're not blind, Dickie," Henry said as he waved his hands around. "Everything's just white . . . like a marshmallow?"

Dickie stood too and put his hands on his hips and looked around.

"Marshmallow . . . land?" Dickie's voice said in awe. "I guess this makes sense as a dreamscape for a 7-year-old."

Henry walked gingerly around the squishy floors to get a feel for it.

"So everything here is made out of marshmallows?" Henry asked.

Dickie reached down and dug his fingers into the floor which stretched before pulling free in his hand. Dickie looked at Henry and popped it into his mouth with a smile.

"I think so," Dickie replied through a mouthful of marshmallows.

Henry reached and grabbed a handful and shoved it into his mouth.

"That's the best-tasting marshmallow I've ever had," Henry declared.

Both boys reached down and grabbed several more handfuls leaving a sticky but delicious film on their fingers and mouths. As he licked his fingers and wiped the residue on his pants, Henry looked around the inside of the dome. He could see several small buildings within the confines of the dome. One was another dome shape—much smaller than the dream dome—with marshmallows stacked one upon the next in an igloo shape. Next to the igloo was a tall tower that created a shadow over a group of marshmallow bicycles with large toothpicks for the frame and handles. The largest part of the dome was what appeared to be a large marshmallow lake with a giant marshmallow carved out to look like a canoe sitting peacefully on the shore.

"This place is amazing," Henry said as he scanned the various marshmallow creations.

"I'm really going to have to hand it to Annabeth Foster from Pascagoula," Dickie replied. "This is quite the imagination."

"Let's go explore!" Henry said as he bounced toward the igloo.

For the next few minutes, Henry and Dickie bounded over to the igloo and crawled inside to find several marshmallow chairs which they promptly sat in.

"This marshmallow chair is way more comfortable than my Dad's old armchair," Dickie said. "Think Annabeth, age 7, would let me take her chair home?"

Henry smiled at his friend's enthusiasm. "I don't think it would fit on the dream train."

They moved to the tower which had 38 marshmallow steps (Dickie counted) spiraling upward toward the top of the dome. The steps were more difficult to traverse than they had expected due to the squishy nature of each step. By the time they reach the top, Henry and Dickie were both winded. While they caught their breath, they looked out not only within the dome but out across the entire dreamscape. The view was as blurry looking out as it had been looking in, but they could see hundreds if not thousands of domes scattered around.

"How are we ever going to find your grandmother with all these domes?" Dickie said quietly.

"I don't know," Henry replied. "Let's keep looking."

Henry and Dickie walked back down the 38 steps of the spiral stairs (which were much easier going down) before walking toward the bicycles that were standing ready near the base of the tower.

"Do you think you can actually ride them?" Dickie asked.

"There's only one way to know," Henry said, nodding toward the two bikes near them.

They each grabbed a bike and tentatively threw a leg over the squishy marshmallow seat and settled there to get used to the balance. Dickie went first and fell over twice as he attempted to ride around the marshmallow courtyard in front of the tower. Henry had somewhat more luck as he successfully made two laps on his bike before giving it up.

"It's like riding on flat tires," Dickie said disappointedly. "I think Annabeth needs to dream up something better."

"It's still pretty cool that it's a marshmallow bike," Henry smirked.

Dickie nodded.

The boys left the bikes behind and headed toward the lake they had seen earlier.

The carved-out marshmallow canoe sat idly by the shore of the lake. The so-called water was filled with the tiniest marshmallows and undulated slowly. Gentle waves pushed their way up the main walkway near where the two boys were standing. From their vantage, the marshmallow lake was much bigger than they had expected.

"Did you know that I am a three-time canoeing badge recipient from summer sessions at Camp Happytown?" Dickie said.

"Three times?" Henry asked. "Why did you get it so many times?"

"I just really liked to canoe," Dickie responded with a smile.

"In that case," Henry said. "Do you care to go canoeing in a lake of marshmallows?"

The boys both laughed at how ridiculous the questions sounded.

"I could think of nothing better," Dickie said, still laughing.

Dickie jumped into the marshmallow canoe causing it to slightly rock side to side. He picked up the oar—which was a long pretzel stick with two large marshmallows on each end—and swung it gently in his hands to get a feel for the weight.

"Push us off and jump in," Dickie directed.

Henry put his hands on the back of the boat and pushed gently causing the boat to slide into the lake. He stepped into the boat and settled in. Dickie pulled the oars through the marshmallow water moving them around the edge of the lake before directing them out into the middle.

"I know they are all marshmallows," Dickie said. "But it feels just like I'm rowing through water."

"I guess it's just the power of imagination," Henry said. "It's like the typical rules don't apply—you can do whatever you want in whatever way you want."

Dickie laid the oar across the marshmallow canoe and breathed in deep. He leaned down and started taking off his shoes and socks.

"What are you doing?" Henry asked.

"I think I'm going to go for a swim," Dickie said. "It feels so much like water it just sounds like fun."

"I don't know," Henry said.

"It's just marshmallows," Dickie replied standing up. "Come in with me and take a dip."

Without further consideration, Dickie jumped into the marshmallow water and began to swim back and forth, joyously laughing at the experience.

"How's it feel?" Henry asked Dickie who had moved further away from the canoe.

"It's cool and refreshing," Dickie yelled. "Just like taking a dip in a real lake in summer."

Henry removed his shoes and socks and stood up to join Dickie in the lake. Dickie was even further away from the canoe than he had been just a moment before.

"Don't swim so far away," Henry yelled.

Henry could just barely make out Dickie's face, but the joy was gone. His friend's face was flushed red which stood out sharply against the sea of white around him.

"Help me, Henry!" Dickie called. "There seems to be a current pulling me away."

"Hang on!" Henry yelled out as he jumped into the marshmallow lake.

Henry could feel the coolness of the marshmallow water surrounding his arms, legs, torso, and neck. He pulled with his arms and propelled himself along toward Dickie. He immediately knew something was wrong as he was moving faster than he would have in regular water. He also felt a downward pull like a riptide tugging on his legs and feet as he neared Dickie. With a few more strokes, Henry was close enough to reach out and grab his friend's arm.

"I'm having trouble keeping my head above the marshmallows," Dickie gasped.

"Hang on! Hang on!" Henry shouting with increasing panic. "Let's see if we can swim toward the shore."

Henry reached out with one hand while holding onto Dickie with the other, but did not make much progress. He could feel Dickie's strength fading as the downward pull got stronger. Henry's breath was quickening as waves of panic were hitting him. Dickie's eyes closed and his head fell beneath the surface of the marshmallow water. Henry hung onto Dickie's arm tightly which was getting heavier by the second. Henry was going to fall beneath the surface as well. He tipped his head back as far as he could and took a large gulp of air as his mouth and nose slipped beneath the surface.

10

The Dream Riders

THE SEA OF WHITE marshmallows was surprisingly dark underneath. Henry could feel himself slowly falling deeper from Dickie's weight and the steady pull from the depths of the lake. He was sure this would be the end for Dickie and himself.

But suddenly Henry felt a tight grip around his wrist and his descent suddenly stopped. The grip tightened and he began to feel himself quickly rising back through the marshmallow water. With a restoration of the ambient light and a giant gulp of air, Henry was yanked free and thrown to the shore of the lake.

He blinked heavily and gasped for air.

Henry sat up on his knees and noticed Dickie's lifeless body lying next to him. Dickie's wet blond curls fell listlessly across his forehead.

"Dickie, Dickie," Henry said as he shook his friend's body. "C'mon man, wake up."

Dickie coughed and then coughed again before he fluttered his eyes and opened them fully.

Henry sighed deeply and rolled back on his bent legs as a shadow fell over Dickie's prone body.

"He'll be okay in a few minutes," a voice said from behind Henry.

Henry looked up and saw a woman standing before them. She wore dark green fatigue pants tucked into shiny black, combat-style boots. Her lightweight canvas jacket hung open exposing a thick bandolier running diagonal across her chest. Henry could see his reflection in the woman's mirrored glasses which contrasted nicely to the woman's silvery hair that was tucked back in a braided red bandana.

"Grandma?" Henry whispered from his knees.

A smile stretched across the woman's face.

"Grandma!" Henry said, jumping to his feet and hugging her tightly.

Henry felt a wave of relief pass through him. The feel of his grandmother's wiry hair against his face and the faint smell of freshly baked cookies was the most comforting thing he had ever felt.

"What are you doing here?" His grandmother asked.

"We got your message," Henry said breathlessly. "We came to find you."

"Who is this we?" she replied. "This soggy young man?"

Henry helped Dickie to his feet. Dickie still looked groggy and discombobulated.

"This is Dickie Dubois," Henry said. "He's my best friend."

Henry's grandmother lowered her mirrored shades down to the edge of her nose and gave Dickie a long look of evaluation. Her dark brown eyes focused intently."

"Nice to meet you, Dickie Dubois," she said, sticking her hand out toward Dickie. "I'm Henry's grandmother."

"Nice to meet you too, Henry's grandmother," Dickie replied as he shook her hand.

"You can call me Leigh," she said with a laugh. "How are you feeling, Dickie?"

"Better, I think," he replied.

"You are very lucky," Leigh said. "It looked like you could have drowned in those marshmallows."

"We thought we were safe," Henry replied. "It was just a dream world made of marshmallows . . . how dangerous could it have been?"

One side of Leigh's mouth curled slightly in a knowing way.

"There is a very fine line between dreams and nightmares," Leigh said reflectively. "Even in a land of marshmallows."

"Speaking of dreams and nightmares," Henry said, "why are you dressed like some sort of guerrilla warrior."

"That's complicated, but I will try to explain," Leigh said. "But first, we need to get moving. We are too exposed here."

"Exposed to what?" Henry asked. "That Xander guy?

"Shush!" Leigh snapped. "Don't say his name too loudly here—you never know who or what is listening."

Henry glanced at Dickie who shrugged.

Leigh led the two boys back up the marshmallow street toward the edge of the dome where Henry and Dickie had pushed through. Leigh walked straight through the boundary without hesitation or hindrance. Dickie stopped at the edge of the dome and looked at Henry with a worried look.

"C'mon boys, we don't have much time," Leigh's muffled voice said from the other side of the dome.

Henry reached out and took Dickie's hand in a much more natural way than when they had tumbled through the barrier before. He took a deep breath and walked forward. He felt the slightly wet sensation again but pushed through to the smiling face of his grandmother. Dickie quickly appeared as well.

"Obviously you found your way here," Leigh said, "but welcome to the land of dreams."

Leigh turned and started walking down the cobbled road between the domes. She was headed away from the Station of Dreams and deeper into the field of dream domes that Henry and Dickie had seen before. Henry and Dickie hurried to keep up with Leigh who was walking faster than her age should have allowed.

"How does this place work?" Henry asked his grandmother breathlessly.

"Each of these domes represents someone's most recent dream," Leigh began. "The dome captures their unique experience—the colors, the shapes, the happiness, and even the fears."

"So that dome back there—the Marshmallowland—was the dream space of . . . Annabeth Foster?" Dickie asked.

"If that's what the sign said," Leigh responded quickly.

Henry watched as they passed dome after dome as Leigh led them through a maze of turns through various streets and several bridges that arched across the same iridescent-colored liquid they had seen earlier.

"If my dreams are *my* dreams," Henry said, "How were we able to access another person's dreams?"

Leigh smiled knowingly at her grandson again before answering.

"When we get somewhere safer I can tell you more," she said, "but understanding how dreams work is the first step."

"I dream almost every night," Dickie said with a grin.

It occurred to Henry that Dickie must have been feeling better. His excitement and full belief in this dream world had seemingly returned.

"That's right," Leigh said. "Most people dream every night whether they can remember it or not. It's an important neurobiological function."

"Neuro . . . what?" Dickie asked.

"Neurobiological," Leigh said, never breaking her stride. "It's the biology of our brains."

"Mom always said dreams were just our imagination running wild," Henry said, glancing at his grandmother."

"That's not quite right," Leigh said. "Our imaginations help us process emotions like joy, fear, happiness, and stress. Our bodies don't always realize it, but our brains are smart enough to know that incredible things happen to us all the time and we don't always actively know it."

Leigh continued their strong pace and moved through a path near dozens more dream domes. Henry saw one that looked like a jungle with limbs and leaves pushing against every inch of the dome's perimeter. Another dome looked like a circus with elephants performing all the acts. The next one looked filled with clouds that flickered and flashed like a summer thunderstorm.

Leigh briefly stopped at a crossroads between four domes. Henry watched as her view lingered slightly on the one to the right. Henry glanced that way and saw that the sign in front of the dome simply said: "Pleasantville, RE112430, Age Unknown." It contained a small wooden bench under the broad, leafless branches of a large tree in front of a dried-out riverbed. Fragile, brown leaves gently blew across the ground, and long spiderwebs ran from the trunk of the tree down to the arms of the bench. The rest of the dome was dark with charcoal gray air that hung heavy all around. Henry was struck with an overwhelming sense of sadness and loneliness and the realization there was nothing pleasant about Pleasantville.

"Grandma?" Henry asked. "Who does this dream dome belong to?"

Leigh glanced back toward the dome Henry was referring to. Her eyes twitched slightly and a wave of sadness washed over her face.

"No one," Leigh said quietly.

Henry watched as his grandmother turned her back to him. He was not sure, but he thought he heard her sniffle quietly. Henry did not understand. They had walked by hundreds of domes that she had ignored, but this one had meant something more to her. She wiped her eyes with the back of her hand and turned back to face the boys.

"C'mon boys—this way," Leigh said pointing off to the left. "We're almost there."

After a few more domes, Leigh and the boys stopped in front of a new dome. Henry noticed that the name and age were written in a text he could not read.

"You two go first," Leigh said, pointing toward the dome.

With less reservation, Henry stepped up to the dome and slowly pushed his way through. He could sense, more than see or hear, that Dickie had followed him.

The dreamscape before them was an impressively wide view of rolling hills with a nearby river snaking through the hills and running past a tall, thick trunked tree that stood on the far side of a wooden bridge. But instead of green grass and blue water, it was all reversed. The knee-high turquoise-colored grass shook from side to side from an invisible wind which gave the appearance of a far-off ocean. Likewise, the river maintained a dark green color that was attractive and mysterious.

"It's all reversed," Dickie said in awe.

"That's right," Leigh said, having followed them through. "Welcome to Reverseland."

She led them down across the waving grass toward the bridge Henry had seen in the distance. From this vantage point, Henry could tell that the tree was not just a tree. It had large circular windows at various locations along its trunk as well as a long rectangular door near its base.

Leigh and Dickie hurried across the bridge, but Henry stopped at its apex to look at the river more closely. The dark green water poured underneath the bridge but ran in an atypical direction. It flowed side to side as if it were a giant liquid coil laid on its side.

"Henry let's go," Leigh said from the other side.

Henry hurried across and stopped in front of what appeared to be a door at the base of the tree. From up close it reminded Henry of an old commercial he had seen when he was younger about a family of gnomes living in a tree baking cookies and cakes.

Leigh reached up and rapped on the center of the door several times in a rhythmic pattern that sounded familiar to Henry. Leigh stepped back and watched the door.

Henry could hear a distinct shuffling behind the door and then a series of clicks as locks were disengaged from the other side. The door swung open to reveal an older man with wild gray locks of gray hair and gold-rimmed glasses perched delicately on the end of a long, beak-like nose.

"I thought you'd never get here," the man said quickly.

"Sorry for the delay," Leigh said. "It's good to see you, Clement."

11

The Sleutel

THE MAN'S EYES FLICKED quickly back and forth between Leigh, Henry, and Dickie.

Much like his grandmother, this man seemed out of place and time. Not only was he hidden in a treehouse next to a green river in a land of blue-colored grass, but he was dressed as a train conductor. He wore faded blue denim overalls with bronze-colored buttons and clips reflecting the ambient light of the dome. Similarly, his head was covered by a stiff black hexagon-shaped hat wrapped in a red band with "Conductor" written across the front. His long silvery locks of hair flowed out from beneath the hat and nearly came to the tops of his shoulders.

"Were you followed?" The man asked as he looked beyond his visitors toward the bridge and the blue grassy hills on the other side of the dream dome.

"We took every precaution," Leigh said quickly.

He took another look at the boys and then back again at Leigh.

"Who are these two?" He asked.

"Clement," Leigh began. "This is my grandson Henry and his friend Dickie."

Clement looked unconvinced by the introductions.

"They are here to help," Leigh pleaded. "They are here with me."

He looked at each boy again with greater detail. Henry wondered if this was how fruit felt at the grocery store before they were picked, bagged, and sent home with a nice family.

Clement nodded and stepped back inside the treehouse.

"What are you waiting for?" He yelled over his shoulder. "It's not safe out there. Come inside."

Leigh directed the boys inside and scanned the horizon before closing the door and securing the locks.

The treehouse was much bigger than Henry had expected. There was a spacious living room with a cooking space at the far end of the room. A wooden ladder rose from the middle of the room to a second floor that Henry assumed was a bedroom.

A comfy-looking leather couch ran along the edge of one side of the room and two wooden rocking chairs sat opposite the couch. A large circular rattan rug covered most of the floor. Odd-shaped boxes were stacked along open spaces between the furniture.

"Boys," Leigh said. "This is my research partner and friend, Dr. Clement Crowne."

Clement nodded at the two boys.

"So you helped my grandmother invent . . . this . . . dream . . . stuff?" Henry asked awkwardly.

"In a manner of speaking, yes," Clement responded. "But we called it . . . "

"Dream riding . . . " Leigh interjected as she sat down in one of the rocking chairs.

"How does it work?" Dickie asked curiously.

Clement sat in the other rocking chair and absently rubbed the back of his neck. He gently tapped the floor with one foot causing the chair to slowly rock back and forth across the edge of the faded rug.

"First, you must understand dreams," Clement said.

"That's right," Henry said. "My grandmother told us about dreams earlier."

"Dreams are a complicated thing," Clement continued, ignoring Henry's rebuttal. "Dreams are real and imaginary at the same time. While we dream we create and perceive our world simultaneously without consciously knowing it, right?"

Dickie and Henry nodded.

"We invented a device . . . ," Clement said.

" . . . a modulator, really," Leigh added.

" . . . that organized an individual dream space for everyone," Clement continued. "The dreamer accesses the space and fills it with their own dreams."

" . . . and those spaces are the domes we saw earlier?" Henry asked.

"Dreamscapes," Leigh said as she sat in the rocking chair next to Clement. "That's what we called the domes—dreamscapes."

Henry let the explanation of the dreamscapes settle over him. He'd been inside two different domes and seen dozens of others, but it still did not seem possible.

"Those dreamscapes can be the most imaginative places," Clement said. "But they can also be incredibly dangerous."

"Don't I know it?" Dickie said.

Clement stared at Dickie with confusion and concern.

"You mentioned a modulator?" Henry asked. "Is that what allows us to walk through other people's dreamscapes?"

Leigh knowingly smiled at Henry as only a proud grandmother can do. "Yes, that's correct."

Henry sheepishly grinned at his grandmother. He was always glad that she was proud of him, but, in the end, he had just guessed. He was still trying to put things together in his mind.

"Is this your house?" Dickie asked Clement.

" . . . and my dreamscape," Clement replied. "I called it Reverseland."

"We saw the sign when we came through," Dickie said, "but it was all jumbled up."

"That darn sign," Clement said as he slapped his knee. "I tried to put it in code, but it always just came out as gobbledygook."

"In code?" Henry asked. "Like the one we passed earlier?"

Henry could see a shadow cross over his grandmother's face. She looked tense and suddenly as old as she actually was. But nearly just as quickly the youthful spirit and vigor returned to her.

"Yes, coded," Clement said as he leaned toward Henry. "When we invented dream riding we decided to give certain dreamscapes a code to protect them from people who might want to do them harm."

"Protect it from whom?" Henry asked.

"Xander Dirwyn for one," Leigh said quickly.

"But I thought he was your partner," Dickie said with a frown.

Neither Leigh nor Clement answered immediately. They rocked in their respective chairs and stared off in the distance. Even within the small space of Clement's tree house, Henry felt like his grandmother and her friend were far off deep into thoughts of another place and time.

"Grandma?" Henry said, resting his hand on her arm. "Are you okay?"

His question—and simple contact—broke her from her thoughts. She covered his hand and gave it a quick squeeze.

"Yes," Leigh said with a quick nod. "Xander Dirwyn was our partner—even a friend—when we started exploring dreamscapes."

"We discovered how to access dreams by accident," Clement said, "but had trouble controlling it. We were just along for the ride."

"That's actually why we started calling ourselves dream riders," Leigh added. "It wasn't until Xander discovered the dream flow and designed the sleutels that we were able to stabilize the dreamspaces."

"What is the dream flow?" Henry asked.

" . . . and what are sleutels?" Dickie echoed.

"I'll show you," Clement grunted.

He stood up and walked across the room and opened a small cabinet built into the walls of the treehouse that Henry had not seen when they had first arrived. The wall swung away to reveal another door with a spinning lock on the outside. Henry watched as Clement's nimble fingers spun the lock left, then right, and back again until a quiet click filled the room and the inner door popped open. Clement reached inside and grabbed something that Henry could not see. Clement closed both doors and returned to his chair.

"This . . . ," Clement said, reaching his hand out toward Henry and Dickie. " . . . is a sleutel."

The item in Clement's hand was a small cylindrical shape about as long as his palm. Its cobalt color seemed to pulse and shimmer.

" . . . and this is my sleutel," Leigh said, taking out a similarly shaped object that was attached to her necklace.

Henry and Dickie looked at the two objects that now sat before them. Leigh's sleutel was a golden yellow color and shimmered. It also had a decorative tree at the top that was made out of silver.

"Is that a Christmas tree on top?" Dickie asked.

Leigh nodded.

"Why a Christmas tree?" Henry asked, looking at his grandmother.

"It was always my favorite holiday," Leigh said with a smile. "It always made me happy so I added it to my sleutel."

For a brief moment, Henry could see Christmas morning clearly in his mind. He had never thought much about it, but he could see his grandmother's smiling face as they opened each present under the soft light of the lit tree.

"I like Christmas trees, too," Dickie said. " . . . but what are sleutels?"

"They are keys," Leigh said.

"Keys to what?" Henry added.

Leigh looked at her grandson again with a concerned expression. Henry could tell she was holding something back. She took a deep breath and exchanged a look with Clement before continuing.

"Back in the day, Xander didn't just discover the sleutels," she said. "He discovered that the source—the energy of all dreams if you will—is something he called the Dream Flow."

"The dream flow?" Henry said, sounding out the words as if to see how they felt on his tongue. "Like the river we saw that flowed between all the domes?"

"That's right," Clement said absently. "Back then, we didn't know where it came from or what it was made of, but it was critical to the whole dream riding thing."

"The dream flow—that river—had to be managed so the flow was consistent to ensure everyone had access to their dreams, freely and safely. We built a machine that sits near the source of the dream flow to help manage the entire dream system. Three keys—or sleutels—mine, Clement's, and Xander's, were used to start the dream machine."

Henry sat back to think about what his grandmother had said. It was like a story out of a history book. It simultaneously felt like the coolest thing he'd ever heard as well as the most unbelievable.

"If the dream machine is on and people can dream, what's the issue?" Henry asked.

"Excellent question," Clement said, nodding quickly.

"Do you remember earlier when we pointed out how important dreams were?" Leigh asked.

Henry and Dickie nodded.

"The critical way dreams help people process their fears and their joys?" Leigh asked again.

Henry looked back and forth between his grandmother and her partner waiting in anticipation for the reveal.

"When we first invented dream riding all three of us saw it that way," Leigh said slowly.

"However, over time Xander began to become disillusioned with the freedom. He suggested that dreams were simply an unnecessary escape and were a waste of people's time and our technology."

"That's stupid," Dickie said flatly. "Dreams are awesome."

"He felt like the dream machine should be shut down and the dream flow destroyed forever," She continued.

"He began to sabotage various parts of the dreamspace," Clement said. "So we decided to split up the sleutels and never speak to each other again."

" . . . and that's where we were until earlier today . . . ," Leigh said quietly.

" . . . until Xander's men came to my home trying to find me and my sleutel," Clement said.

"Wait, wait," Dickie said, holding up his hands. "Why does he need the sleutels if the dream machine is already on? Can't he just go to the machine and turn it off?"

For the first time since they had arrived to Reverseland, a broad smile spilled over the faces of Leigh and Clement.

"That's the beauty of our design," Clement said. "To protect the dreams, we built the machine in such a way to require all three sleutels to start *or* stop the machine."

Dickie leaned back in his seat with a look of surprise and understanding. "Very smart."

"So that's why Xander's been chasing you?" Henry asked. "He wants to steal your two sleutels to shut down the dream machine?"

Leigh and Clement nodded solemnly.

"We can't let him do that!" Dickie said with a clap.

"So what do we do now?" Henry asked.

But Henry's question was interrupted by three loud bangs on the door to Clement's treehouse.

"You are surrounded," A voice yelled from the other side of the door. "Bring the sleutels out and you won't be harmed . . . much."

12

The Root Cellar

"HE FOUND US!" CLEMENT said as he jumped from his chair leaving it rocking in his wake.

"Who?" Dickie squeaked. "Xander?"

The banging on the door started again. Henry noticed that the hinges on the door shook causing dust to fall to the ground like snow.

"Is there any other way out of here?" Leigh said to Clement.

"Clement? Leigh?" A voice said from outside the door. "It's me—Xander. Let's make this easy. Just hand over the yellow and blue sleutels and I'll be on my way."

"We'll never give them to you!" Henry yelled at the door.

There was a pause from the banging and movement outside.

"Who might we have on the other side of the door?" Xander called out from beyond the treehouse. "Who's your . . . young friend?

Henry's blood ran cold. The outside voice dripped with malice. Xander had seemed like the bad guy from a book or movie, but now his presence felt real, filled with all the dimensions of hate and evil.

"Henry?" Leigh said, placing her hand on his shoulder. "We need to go."

"Where are we going?" Henry asked fearfully, thinking about the ominous voice from beyond the door.

"The root cellar," Clement said.

"Follow me," Leigh said as she took his hand.

Leigh, Henry, and Dickie followed Clement across the room of the treehouse to the pounding sound of the door being pushed to its limits. Clement slid a large black and white rug to the side revealing a small door on the floor. He tugged on a small wooden circular handle pulling the door open.

Henry was overwhelmed by the scent of wet dirt and rotting wood that emanated from the opened door. Beyond the smell, Henry could see the rungs of a small wooden ladder running into the darkness beyond.

"You're going to need this," Clement said as he pressed a small flashlight into Henry's hand.

A loud crack echoed throughout the treehouse as the front door began to splinter from whatever was happening outside.

"They are breaking through!" Dickie screamed.

"Everyone, follow me," Clement said as he stepped into the hole and descended the ladder.

Clement disappeared down the hole with Dickie quickly following. Henry clicked his flashlight on and held it between his teeth as he stepped onto the rungs of the ladder and plunged into the darkness. Henry stepped down two, four, then six rungs with only the light of his flashlight holding back the darkness of the room and the rising tightness of fear in his chest.

Henry's feet touched the bottom and he felt it give slightly, but otherwise held his weight. His grandmother stepped off the ladder seconds later. Henry took the flashlight from between his teeth and swung it around to light up the room better. Henry could see that the walls, floor, and ceiling were all the same dark brown color and glistened slightly in the torchlight. Clement's head was mere inches from the ceiling.

"Where are we?" Henry's voice echoed.

"We are in the roots of my treehouse," Clement said.

"The roots?" Henry asked skeptically. "How can we be in the root of your treehouse?"

"That's the power of dreams, darling," Leigh replied. "It's a root cellar."

"If we follow the root it should take us to the only water source in Reverseland—the green river."

With their flashlights dancing across the walls of the hollow root, Clement led the foursome down the path and away from Xander and his goons. Clement walked quickly, but the walls of the root narrowed such that after a few minutes, Clement was nearly bent in half. Henry could feel the wetness of the walls dampen his hair which was now brushing the top of the root.

After a few more minutes, the tunnel had squeezed so tight Henry was sure they would be trapped. Clement was crawling on his stomach while Leigh, Henry, and Dickie crawled on their hands and knees.

"We're there," Clement said from the front of their line.

"Where is that?" Dickie said.

From Henry's perspective, all he could see was the end of the root tunnel. The walls all converged at what looked like a wall.

Clement turned on his side and awkwardly turned his body where his leg faced the end of the tunnel. Henry's fear was rising. He looked over his shoulder wondering what would be waiting for them back in the treehouse if they all had to turn around.

"Are we stuck?" Dickie said with panic in his voice.

To Henry's surprise, Clement answered Dickie by kicking the wall at the end of the root.

Henry looked at Dickie whose face was pinched in concern with panic creeping in around the edges.

After several more kicks, Henry smelled something different and felt a slight breeze across his face. The strong smell of earth and dirt was still present, but Henry was certain he could smell the faint, but comforting aroma of roasted marshmallows.

"I've broken through," Clement said, wiping his hand across his brow leaving a smear of dirt. "A little bit more and we'll be able to squeeze through."

Henry breathed deeply trying to ignore the growing muscle cramps in his legs that were inevitable in the tight space.

After another few minutes of digging, Clement wiggled through the tight hole widening more as his hips pulled through. Henry and Dickie quickly followed with Leigh at their heels. Henry remained on his knees feeling the cooler air blow across his face and arms bringing blissful relief. The sound of the green river could be heard down the hill of tall blue grass that waved around.

Henry could hear the sounds of their breath mingle with the quiet sounds of the dancing grass. Off in the distance Xander's men moved in and around Clement's treehouse. An occasional crashing sound could be heard as well. Henry looked at Clement's dirt-strewn face which looked sad.

"I don't think they've seen us," Leigh said. "We must quietly work our way down to the river."

"Hey stop!" A voice yelled in the distance. "They are trying to escape."

Leigh frowned. "So much for the quiet part—RUN!"

All four of them stood up and began running in the direction of the sound of the river that Henry had heard earlier. The long blades of grass brushed past Henry leaving small scratches on his arms. His legs ached from having been in the cramped space of the root for so long.

Clement had pulled ahead of Leigh and the boys. "Hurry boys—they are coming!"

Henry glanced back toward the treehouse and Xander's advancing men. Clement had been right. There were dozens of men tearing through the cobalt grass leaving paths like ghosts.

Henry could now not only hear the river but see it rushing along at the edge of the grass. As they passed the top of the last hill, Henry saw two boats tied neatly to the edge of the river.

Henry glanced over his shoulder again but stumbled and fell to his knees tearing a hole in the pants he was wearing.

"Hurry!" Clement yelled. "They are almost on us."

They may have been in a dreamscape, but Henry was filled with fear. Panic was settling into his bones, but then a hand appeared before his face. His grandmother was reaching down to help him. Their eyes locked and the calmness of her eyes was so comforting. She nodded, helped him to his feet, and quickly pulled him in the direction of the boats.

As they ran the final few feet they saw where Clement and Dickie had pushed off in their boat and were already moving down the river of green water. Henry could feel the steady pull of the water as he and Leigh jumped into the second boat and pushed off. Henry looked back at his grandmother's face which had broken into a grin, but which was now slowly fading. Henry could tell something was wrong, but could not understand. They had escaped the house and made the river, what could go wrong now?

"Henry, look out!" She yelled as she pointed at him.

Henry felt a strong tug and was pulled off his seat toward the stern of the boat. One of Xander's men had managed to jump on the back of the boat when they had pushed off. He held Henry's shoulders and seemed to be trying to pull him from the boat. Henry could feel the tight grip of the man's hands and feel his ragged breathing, but could not see his face. Henry could only see his grandmother's face which seemed to be shifting again. The fear that had replaced her earlier happiness had left and was replaced with a steely resolve.

"Let . . . go . . . of . . . my . . . grandson!" Leigh growled as she stood up in the bow of the small boat. "Henry, hold on to something!"

As Henry reached over and grabbed the side of the boat, he felt the boat begin to tip from side to side. His grandmother's standing position and shifting weight from side to side was causing the boat to tip with increasing degree. The weight of the man holding Henry was shifting, but his grip was still tight.

With one more violent tip, Henry finally felt the man's hold slip as he slid off the side of the boat and into the green waters. Unfortunately for Henry, the change in weight caused the boat to continue to tip rather than return to its balanced form. Both Henry and his grandmother fell out of the boat and plunged into the darkness of the green river of Reverseland.

13

The Green River

HENRY GULPED AT THE air as his face broke the surface of the water. The current of the green river was much stronger than he had anticipated. He glanced around and saw his grandmother floating on the surface as well. The hired henchman was thrashing around violently, bewildered and confused. The capsized boat was well ahead of them and was quickly floating away.

Henry could feel his wet clothes and shoes weighing him down in the river. He had to paddle quickly with his hands to keep afloat.

"Henry!" Leigh yelled. "Try to swim to the shore."

Henry's mouth and nose briefly dipped below the water line. But he quickly recovered and nodded at his grandmother. He mimicked her actions by using his arms and legs to aim toward the shore on the far side. The henchman calmed slightly and was trying to follow them. The river was getting faster the further they traveled.

His grandmother got to the shore first and grabbed a series of embedded rocks. Henry was pushed slightly further down the river but managed to grab hold of a similar set of rocks.

"You okay?" Leigh yelled over the noise of the river.

Henry smiled at her. "I'm just fi-"

But Henry felt a firm tug from behind and lost his grip on the wet rocks. He was again plunged back into the depths of the green water. He could feel a tight grip around his arm. His body rose to the surface and he was face to face with the henchman who had grabbed him earlier. A long pointed, wart-covered nose stuck out through the man's matted wet hair. Henry struggled, but the man's grip seemed to tighten.

"Give up!" the ugly henchman yelled. "I've got you–"

For the third time in the last few minutes, Henry felt another tug on the back of his shirt but this time his journey was upward. He felt his torso and then his legs quickly pull free from the river. The quick change in direction caused the henchman to lose his grip and slip back into the current and float away from Henry.

Henry landed with a thud on a hard wooden surface. He wiped his face with the back of his wet sleeve before looking around. Clement and Dickie sat on their knees around Henry looking at him with cause and concern.

"Are you okay?" Clement asked. "I had to pull you from the river."

Henry blinked several times.

"You pulled me from the river?" Henry replied.

"Absolutely he did," Dickie chirped. "It was awesome—he snatched you right out with his bare hands."

"It seemed prudent," Clement said flatly.

" . . . as will moving along from here," Leigh said, walking near them along the dock. "Xander's men won't let this stop them. We need to find somewhere safer."

Clement—as the owner of the Reverseland dreamscape and thus the best navigator—led Leigh, Henry, and Dickie over the rolling blue grass hills and toward the edge of the dome. Henry's sodden clothes felt heavy and burdensome as they walked.

As they neared the edge of the dome, they all slipped through the transparent surface. As Henry slid through, he felt slightly squeezed like a sponge getting wrung out. When he fully emerged, the weight of his wet clothes was gone. He ran his hands along his sleeves, pants, and hair to find them all dry.

"Let's head off this way," Leigh said, taking the lead.

"Grandma?" Henry asked as they walked along. "Why am I dry?"

"What do you mean?" She asked distractedly as she looked at the path ahead of them.

"My clothes were wet back in Reverseland from where we fell into the river," he said quickly. "But now they are dry—completely dry. It's like it never happened."

"That's one of the characteristics of dreaming," Leigh said. "The conditions of the dreamer and thus the dream and dreamscape cannot escape the confines of the dream."

"In other words," Clement added, "if you're wet in my dream, you can't be wet outside of that dream."

Henry nodded but was not sure he fully understood. He was, however, very pleased to be dry.

Now that they were outside of Reverseland, Leigh took the lead and led them back along the path they had used earlier. They came to the T-shaped split on the road where the dark and dusty dome had been. Henry glanced at it again and felt the same sense of sadness as before. It was like he was looking at a dream at sunset ready to fade away forever.

"Grandma?" Henry said as they passed the dome. "What's wrong with that dome?"

Leigh glanced over seemingly unaware of what Henry was asking about. That same look passed over her face that Henry had seen earlier, but it just as quickly passed.

"We don't have time to talk about it," Leigh said. "We need to find shelter."

"Do you think Xander's henchman will find us again?" Dickie whispered. "We barely escaped back there."

"You're right," Henry whispered in turn. "But we can't let Xander turn off this place—it's too valuable."

Leigh, Clement, Henry, and Dickie walked for several more minutes following various paths running near an ever-increasing number of dreamscapes of various colors, shapes, and names.

"I think this is our best place to hide," Leigh said as she stopped in front of a dark, green-colored dome.

14

Suzie's Dinner

THE SIGN IN FRONT of the dome said, "Suzie's Dinner, Suzie Newman, Age 6 ¾." Henry remembered seeing the dome earlier. Through the opaque thickness of the dome, there appeared to be large green leaves everywhere, giving it a distinctive jungle vibe.

As they walked through the edge of the dome, Henry's vision was obscured by dark green foliage and light-colored vines in every direction and he was overwhelmed by a fragrant smell that was both sharp and familiar somehow. He could hear the shake and rattle of leaves and breaking branches as Dickie, Clement, and his grandmother entered the dome as well. After several steps, Henry and the others broke through the foliage into a large opening where a slow brook meandered over and around large, round, dark brown rocks.

"It's . . . red," Dickie said. "It's a red creek."

"Indeed," Clement said, looking around. "A slow red creek."

Leigh led the group to a cluster of large brown rocks near the edge of the slow-moving red creek. Clement and Leigh sat on adjacent rocks. They immediately put their heads together and began to talk quietly. Henry and Dickie took a seat on nearby rocks.

"I'd say this place is weird," Henry said. "But after a land of marshmallows and rivers of various colors . . . . I'm beginning to think this place is just like a dream."

Dickie laughed at his friend.

"You might be right," Dickie said after the laughter had passed. "What is Suzie's Dinner?"

"Like this red creek?" Henry asked. "It's slow, thick, and sluggish . . . almost like a sauce."

"Exactly!" Dickie replied. "How about these rocks?"

"They do seem less firm—almost squishy—than I would have expected," Henry said as he bounced slightly on the rock.

"They are round, too," Dickie said. "Perfectly round—there is no way that shape is natural."

The two boys sat together, resting, as Clement and Leigh continued to quietly plan their next steps. This particular dreamscape was very quiet and Henry realized this was the first time they had slowed down since arriving on the train. He was not sure how long it had been since they had arrived. His legs ached, his mouth was dry, but most of all he was hungry.

"That's it!" Henry said, slapping his knee. "I'm hungry."

"Say what?" Dickie said, confused.

Henry jumped to his feet and walked back toward the foliage that he had walked through earlier. Dickie quickly followed trying to keep up with his friend. Henry grabbed a handful of leaves and pushed them up against his nose and inhaled deeply before a wide smile broke out across his face.

"Smell this?" Henry said, pulling leaves free and shoving them toward Dickie. "What does that smell like to you?"

Dickie inhaled quickly and shook his head.

"It's lettuce!" Henry said. "It's like a forest of lettuce."

Dickie smelled the leaves again, inhaling slower this time. After a brief pause, Dickie took a large bite from the handful of leaves before spitting them back out on the ground.

"Oh, no," Henry said. "Was I wrong?"

"No, you were right," Dickie said as he scraped his tongue. "I just remembered how much I hate lettuce. It reminds me of all those times my mother made me sit at the dining table trying to gag down one bit of lettuce from her salad at a time. The only re-deeming quality was the big plate of spaghetti, tomato sauce, and meatballs that followed it."

"That's it!" Henry said as he grabbed Dickie by the shoulders.

"What?" Dickie asked, confused again.

Henry ran past his friends back toward the creek where Leigh and Clement were sitting. Dickie scrambled to follow his friend's movements. Henry fell to his knees next to the creek and looked back at Dickie who did the same. Henry locked eyes with Dickie and nodded before dipping his cupped hands into the creek and filling them with the thick red fluid. He raised it to his lips and took a big slurp, nearly emptying his hands.

He leaned back on his heels and watched Dickie repeat his actions. Dickie took his sip and looked back at Henry with a huge grin.

"It's tomato sauce!" Dickie said as he wiped his mouth with the back of his hand. "It's warm and delicious and tasty."

" . . . and if that is tomato sauce . . . ," Henry said with a smile. "I bet these rocks are actually meatballs."

Dickie's eyes widened and he reached for the nearby rock. He placed his hands wide on the surface and slowly pinched his fingers back together until they dug into the rock and pulled free a handful of rock in each hand. He reached over to Henry and passed a handful to him. They looked at each other, nodded, and took a bite of their respective rock pieces.

"Yep," Dickie said through a mouthful of rock. "That's definitely a meatball."

"The only thing we're missing is the spaghetti noodles," Henry said with a smile.

Clement and Leigh stood up and walked over to the boys who were tearing off pieces of meatball and dipping them in the tomato sauce river.

"It's time to go," Leigh said. "We have a plan to head toward the—"

"Stop where you are!" A voice yelled from the lettuce on the far side of the creek.

"Run, boys!" Clement yelled.

15

The Ravine

WITHOUT FURTHER DELAY, THEY broke into a run following the path of the tomato sauce creek. Lettuce slapped their faces and arms where the vegetation grew close to the creek. Henry could hear the heavy footsteps of Xander's henchmen running after them.

"Run as fast as you can," Leigh hissed. "They are gaining on us."

Henry could feel the sides of his chest ache as he ran faster than he ever had before. Dickie stayed with him as did Clement and his grandmother. He could see a change in light ahead as the flow of the tomato sauce disappeared behind a curve. Two more steps and he was almost there. He reached out and swatted the lettuce leaf and some long vines to the side and skidded to a stop.

Small pebbles and loose dirt tumbled over the edge into a wide ravine. The tomato sauce creek had not disappeared behind a curve but had fallen off a cliff forming a waterfall of deliciousness. Several large branches hung across the ravine. Taste aside, the four of them were trapped. The sounds of the henchmen were growing louder.

Henry looked across the ravine. Several large branches fell out across the gap but were too far to grab with their hands. The ground was flat on the other side and sloped away quickly. Henry was sure they could escape quickly if they could get to the other side.

"What do we do?" Dickie said, echoing Henry's thoughts. "This ravine is too far to jump—we'd never make it."

Henry just shook his head and shrugged. His mind was completely blank.

"If we had a rope maybe we could swing across the gap," Dickie suggested quickly.

"We don't have a rope, but . . . ," Henry said as he walked quickly back into the foliage.

"Where are you going, Henry?" Leigh shouted. "You're running back toward them!"

"Whatever you are doing, Henry," Dickie yelled, "hurry up!"

The lettuce leaves began to shake and stir in front of them and shouts of the henchmen could be heard. Clement moved in front of Dickie and shifted his weight to confront the henchmen if they broke through. Dickie gasped as the leaves separated and Henry broke back through.

"We don't have rope, but we do have spaghetti noodles!" Henry said as he held up several rolls of tan-colored tubes. "It is hanging everywhere in the foliage."

"How did you know it was there?" Clement asked quickly.

"I saw it earlier when we were running, but I didn't know what it was," Henry said with a smile. "It makes perfect sense now—it's Suzie's Dinner! Spaghetti with meatballs and a side salad."

Henry smiled at Dickie whose face broke out in a huge grin.

"Let's go," Leigh said. "Let's see if you are right about spaghetti as a rope."

Each one grabbed a length of spaghetti noodle and stepped up to the edge of the ravine. Leigh and Henry looped their spaghetti ropes and slung them out and over the branch hanging above the ravine. The noodle wrapped around the branch and held tight.

"Ready?" Leigh asked Henry.

Henry took a breath, closed his eyes, and nodded.

Henry and his grandmother leaned out testing their weight against the noodle. Leigh swung across first, successfully landing on the far side of the ravine. Henry exhaled deeply, happy his grandmother had made it. She nodded at Henry to start his swing. He stepped off the edge and felt the noodle stretch with his weight. As it swung toward the far side, Henry reached out his hand toward his grandmother who snagged his hand pulling him successfully to the far side.

Henry turned to see Dickie standing on the edge. Henry locked eyes with Dickie who looked scared and exhilarated at the same time. Clement stood several feet behind Dickie.

"C'mon, Dickie," Henry yelled, waving his hand. "You can do it."

But as the words came out of his mouth, Henry noticed movement in the vegetation behind Clement. Before he could shout a warning, two of Xander's henchmen broke through the wall of vegetation and grabbed Clement by the arms.

"We've got you now," the henchmen on the left said with a leer.

Clement wiggled and wrestled, but was unable to pull free.

"Go Dickie!" Clement yelled. "You must swing now."

Henry watched the entire scene as if it was in slow motion. Dickie leaned out as one of the henchmen reached his arm out and swung toward Dickie but missed as the noodle stretched tight and Dickie slipped away. Henry reached out in anticipation as Dickie swung toward him and his grandmother. Just like Henry had done minutes earlier, Dickie reached out and grabbed Henry's hand, but his fingers slipped free just as quickly. Dickie began to fall back away from Henry spinning out of control.

"No!" Henry yelled.

As Dickie's reverse swing approached the side, he tried to kick at the henchman to keep him away but slipped from the noodle rope and fell hard to the ground. The second henchman dragged Dickie roughly to his feet. Dickie grimaced in pain. Dickie and Clement stood next to each other both captured.

Xander stepped free of the foliage and walked toward where Clement was being held. He roughly dug into Clement's pockets until he found what he was looking for—the second sleutel. Xander walked to the edge of the ravine and held up the two sleutels—his and the one he had just taken from Clement—for Henry and Leigh to see.

"Grandma!" Henry yelled. "They have Dickie."

"Grandma?" Xander questioned. "How interesting, Leigh."

"I'll never give you my sleutel," Leigh said more confidently than Henry could believe.

"Tsk, tsk," Xander replied through gritted teeth. "Of course you will."

"Let my friend go," Henry yelled.

"Be quiet, boy," Xander replied, still looking at Leigh. "Your grandmother and I were talking."

"Go, Leigh," Clement said as he struggled against the henchmen. "Go and hide and never give it to him."

Henry glanced at his grandmother and saw for the first time what he thought was fear. Xander, on the other hand, was smiling a vicious grin that reminded Henry of a jackal.

"Go ahead and hide," Xander said. "We won't chase you anymore."

"Why not?" Leigh said slowly.

"Because if you don't give me your sleutel, there will be . . . ," Xander said as he grabbed Dickie and dragged him to the edge of the ravine, " . . . consequences."

"No!" Leigh said. "Don't hurt the boy."

"Then bring me the sleutel," Xander snapped. "Plain and simple."

The muscles in Leigh's jaw clenched several times before she placed her hand on Henry's shoulder and pushed him away from the edge.

"Grandma?" Henry asked. "What about Dickie and Clement?"

"We'll figure something out," She began. "But we need to be somewhere else, somewhere safer."

Henry reluctantly relented and they walked down the hill away from the ravine. Henry glanced over his shoulder. His best friend looked more afraid than he had ever seen him.

"When you're ready," Xander called out, "you'll know where to find me."

16

Space Pirate

THE VOICES OF THE henchmen echoed in Henry's ears as his grandmother led them down the path on the far side of the tomato sauce river. His nerves were frayed. This constant shifting in and out of fear and panic was exhausting.

Leigh led Henry down a hill and back out of the dome onto the main road between the domes. Henry was surprised at how fresh the air smelled outside of the dome. He had gotten used to the strong aromatic smell of the noodles, sauce, meatballs, and lettuce that perfumed the dome. The air not only smelled fresher, but was somehow lighter as well.

But then the reality of the situation fell on Henry like bricks from the sky. Xander Dirwyn had not only captured his best friend but was now in possession of two of the three sleutels his grandmother had said controlled everyone's access to the dreamscapes.

"Grandma?" Henry asked as he followed her down the path. "Where are we going?"

"The only place we have left," She replied without looking back.

Henry frowned at her answer, but after all they had experienced, he was willing to have faith she would guide them somewhere safe.

"What are we going to do?" Henry asked. "We can't give him the third sleutel, but they have Dickie and Clement."

"I'm well aware," Leigh said dismissively.

Henry watched her as she walked quickly past a variety of domes, dipping between others and then finally coming to a stop in front of a dome that was such a dark blue it almost looked black. Small silvery white beads were scattered across the dome's surface and flickered on and off as if they were winking.

A rectangular white sign in front of the dome read: "Maddy Leigh, age unknown."

"Who's Maddy Leigh?" Henry asked.

To Henry's surprise, Leigh smiled at him.

"Me," she replied as she walked through the surface of the dome.

Without any further instruction, Henry stepped forward as well. He felt the regular tug of the semi-transparent border of the dome wall pull against his head, shoulder, and arms before pulling through on the other side.

Henry was on a long metal platform like a pier that ran out into the largest void he had ever seen. It looked like pictures of space (or at least some dream version of it).

The dome looked like an inky black galaxy filled with thousands of twinkling stars. Among the stars, there were also several disproportionately sized planets of various colors and shapes. The largest—a lavender spinning sphere—had a silver-colored ring running around its midsection.

"What do you think?" Leigh asked.

"What is this place?" Henry asked, returning the question.

"It's my dreamscape," she said looking out. "I wanted it to have a fancy name—maybe something in Latin—but I just call it My Galaxy."

Henry was impressed as this was the largest dreamscape he had seen yet. It truly was a world within the world, but Henry's concern for Dickie and Clement hung on him like a weight.

"It's lovely, but how are we going to get our friends back?" Henry said looking back at his grandmother.

Henry watched as the reverie of returning to a place of comfort slowly fell away from his grandmother's face.

"I'm not sure yet," she said, frowning before dropping her eyes, "but here comes our ride."

"Our ride?" Henry asked.

Henry walked up next to his grandmother who was waving at a boat approaching the pier from deeper in the dreamscape. It was a ship in space, but not a spaceship exactly. It looked more like an ancient wooden boat with large white sails magically deployed in the vacuum of the dreamspace. Two large mechanical motors were attached to the back. It pulled to a stop hovering gently near the edge of the pier.

A loud bang echoed through the dream space as a long wooden plank fell from the ship and landed on the pier. A series of loud, slow thumps echoed through Henry's ears as a figure appeared. The figure was so odd and so surreal that it could only belong in a child's dream. Henry would have described the man as a pirate, but that did not do the figure justice. Gold buttons glittered against the man's charcoal gray jacket. His tricorn hat was the same color as the jacket and had the ghoulish shape of a skull on the front. A similar skull sat atop a twisted cane that was tucked under the gnarled fingers of his hand.

"'Ello, Leigh," the man said with a brusque accent. "It's good ta see ya again."

Henry gasped as the man stepped closer and into the brighter light of the pier. This man—this space pirate—was missing a significant portion of his left leg. Where his leg should have been, lines of glowing electrical current sizzled and bridged from a metal plate covering his hip down to his black booted foot. Additionally, Henry could now see that one of the man's eyes was covered by a riveted black metal eyepatch.

The pirate seemed to notice Henry's gawking.

"What 'er ya lookin' at, boy?" The man said gruffly.

Henry stared blankly at the man and then his grandmother, unable to put words together.

Henry felt immediate relief as his grandmother stepped forward and grabbed his flustered shoulder.

"Henry," Leigh said, looking at the man. "This is Captain Lectro. Captain Lectro, this is my grandson Henry."

"Are you a space pirate?" Henry asked.

Captain Lectro leaned forward and took Henry's slowly outreached hand causing his beard to make a soft jingling sound. With his face so close, Henry could easily make out that Captain Lectro's beard was mostly made up of various electrical wires, connectors, and plugs.

Henry swallowed heavily. "Why . . . why do they call you Captain Lectro?"

Captain Lectro narrowed his one good eye and stroked this odd beard as he considered the question.

"Perhaps it's me' metal eye patch?" He pondered. "Or maybe it's my beard of electrical cords?"

Henry glanced at his grandmother who seemed to be smirking.

"Or perhaps it's me' leg?" Captain Lectro asked with a tilted grin. He tapped his leg with the skull cane causing smarks to fly in all directions. "We may just never know."

"Enough with the show, Captain Lectro," Leigh interrupted. "We are in trouble and need help."

"Of course," Captain Lectro said. "Follow me to my ship and we'll be on our way."

17

Ari

CAPTAIN LECTRO STOOD AT the helm of his ship—affectionately named the S.S. Resistance—slowly turning the large wooden wheel of the helm to adjust their path. Henry could feel the slight vibration of the ship under his feet as they sailed deeper into the darkness of his grandmother's dreamscape.

"Ahoy, Leigh," Captain Lectro called out. "We're nearin' 'ur requested destination."

Leigh nodded next to Captain Lectro but continued to gaze toward the lavender-colored orb Henry had noticed earlier.

Henry had assumed it would get larger the closer they got to it, but it had remained the same size—another unique trick of the dream space. Henry's gut roiled as he realized Dickie would have enjoyed this dreamscape. He wondered if Dickie was okay and whether Xander Dirwyn and his men had harmed him or Clement in any way.

"I'm worried about them too," Leigh's voice said, reading his thoughts.

Henry had not realized she had joined him at the rail.

"Are we heading to that planet over there?" Henry asked.

"You guessed it," she nodded. "But technically I think it's a moon."

Henry returned his gaze to the moon and the vast space of this dome.

"Grandma?" Henry asked as he placed his hands on the ship's rail. "How is any of this possible?"

"What do you mean?" she asked, turning to look at him.

"These dreamscapes seem so real, but so impossible at the same time," Henry blurted out. "I knew dreams were endless, but I'm overwhelmed by everything we've seen. I'm overwhelmed by being in these dreamscapes and experiencing other people's dreams."

Leigh slowly nodded but never looked away.

"It seems weird to spend so much time in dreams," Henry said with a wave of his hand. "So much time away from your real life."

Leigh breathed in deeply and pursed her lips as she exhaled slowly.

"That's an excellent observation, Henry," she said, squeezing his hand. "When we arrive I'll explain everything."

Captain Lectro flew the S.S. Resistance closer and closer until he pulled up to the silver ring Henry had seen earlier. He had assumed they were made up of celestial elements like he had been taught in science class, but close up it appeared to be metal walkways that ran around the lavender moon. Henry followed his grandmother down the plank which had been lowered with a clang.

"Thanks again for the lift," Leigh said, waving back toward Captain Lectro.

"O'course, me dear," Captain Lecto called back from the helm. "I'm always 'appy to 'elp a friend in need."

The S.S. Resistance pulled away from the metal rail of the moon, propelled again by the wind of dreams unseen.

Leigh turned toward the lavender moon which up close was poxed with various small valleys and fissures. She stepped toward one of the larger spots and placed her hand in the middle of the crater with her fingers splayed in all directions. A glowing white line slowly outlined her fingers. Henry glanced at his grandmother's face, but she seemed calm and serene in the soft lavender glow. With a soft click and a hiss of air, the circle of the crater slid up and to the side revealing a hallway running deep into the moon. Leigh signaled to Henry to follow her as she walked into the tunnel.

Henry stepped into the moon and felt the ground squish slightly beneath his feet. The hall had a recognizably pungent smell that made him think of his grandmother's kitchen.

"Why does the moon smell like cheese?" Henry sniffed.

Leigh let out a laugh that echoed softly in the tunnel. "Because this moon is made of cheese."

"Really?" Henry quipped.

"When I was a little girl my grandmother would read me a story about the moon being made of cheese," Leigh said with a nostalgic grin. "It always made me happy to think about it, so I made my dreamscape a moon made of cheese."

Henry could see a light up ahead. He followed his grandmother for another minute or two before they stepped into an open room. After a glance, Henry recognized it immediately.

"It's your living room!" Henry exclaimed.

Leigh nodded and grinned sheepishly.

A long green couch ran along the far wall with tall lamps projecting a soft yellow light from each end. A brown rocking chair sat to one side and an old (yet somehow incredibly enticing) brown leather chair sat at the other end of the room. The same picture of a vase of lilies hung on a wall behind the couch near a small red glass dish overflowing with shiny-colored wrappers of various candies.

There was even a window that overlooked a green lawn. A window and lawn that clearly could not exist inside a moon made of cheese. Beneath the window was a table filled with snow globes just like Henry remembered. As he glanced down at the snow globes, he noticed they were all filled with Christmas trees. Some were tall and skinny while others were squatty and fat. Each—regardless of size or shape—was decorated with strings of tiny lights and lots of little ball ornaments.

"I never could get enough," Leigh said. "I just loved Christmas trees."

Henry glanced at his grandmother who was slowly rubbing the tree-topped sleutel that hung from her neck.

The rocking chair creaked as Leigh took a seat. Henry sat down in the leather chair opposite his grandmother. He felt his body slowly sag into the soft leather. A wave of relief washed over his tired muscles. This was another paradox for Henry. The soft leather of the chair brought wonderful relief to his tired body. It was almost as real as he remembered from his grandmother's real living room. But not everything. This chair was missing a small tear in the armrest that Henry had picked at as a child.

The creak of Leigh's chair filled the room as they both sat thinking their respective thoughts.

"I used to come here with your Grandpa," Leigh said as she rocked her chair rhythmically. "Do you remember much about him?"

"Not a whole lot," Henry said quietly.

"That's what I figured," Leigh said. "He's been sick for a long time."

Henry closed his eyes and focused on what he did remember of his grandfather.

"I remember he was tall and strong and loved to laugh at a good joke," Henry said as he opened his eyes.

Henry looked at his grandmother and thought her eyes were twinkling.

"That's right," Leigh said, nodding. "He had a laugh that would fill a room."

Leigh reached over and picked up a framed photo of a young man with his arm around a young woman. It was hard to tell, but Henry was pretty sure the woman smiling was his grandmother.

"His name was Ari," Leigh said as she placed the picture back on the table. "But I called him Ship."

Henry watched as a sense of sadness seemed to weigh down her face. The smile had been pushed away, extinguishing the sparkle he had just seen.

"We used to come to one of our dreamscapes nearly every day," Leigh said quietly.

"Why did you come in here so often?" Henry asked. "Why not just hang out together in the real world?"

"Things just always seemed better here," she said. "Colors seemed brighter, food tasted better, noises more vibrant, but I also liked the fact that I never had to work—no cooking and no cleaning."

"Did you always meet here in this dreamscape?"

"Most of the time we did," she said quickly. "But sometimes we would visit his dreamscape and just sit on a park bench under an old oak tree and watch a narrow river float by."

The picture of his grandfather's dreamscape triggered something in Henry's mind. It sounded familiar to him.

"That's quite the image," Henry said absently.

"Indeed," Leigh replied. "He called it Pleasantville."

"Pleasantville?!" Henry blurted out. "Wasn't that the name of that dome we've passed that's all dark, dusty, and deserted?"

Leigh's lip quivered and her face tightened.

"Grandma?" Henry asked, stepping toward her. "You okay?"

Leigh squeezed her eyes tight and wiped away the tears that had run down her cheeks. She nodded quickly and forced her face to smile at Henry.

"That was his dreamscape," she said.

"What happened to it?" Henry said, kneeling next to his grandmother. "It doesn't look anything like you described."

"No, you're right," She said. "As your grandfather's sickness progressed, he changed too. When a person changes, their dreamscape changes."

Henry gently placed his hand over his grandmother's hand and squeezed. He knew his grandfather had been sick for a long time, but had never thought much about what was happening in his mind or whether he was still able to dream. It was clear that he had been a special man and that his grandmother had loved him dearly.

"I miss him, Henry," Leigh whispered.

"This place is obviously very special," Henry said.

Leigh nodded, still overcome by their conversation.

"Not just this space," Henry said as he waved his hand around the room. "But the entire space—the collective importance of all of these domes—these dreamscapes."

Henry was feeling energized. For the first time, since they had arrived he was beginning to understand the lay of this magical land. The beginning of a plan was developing in his mind.

"We must protect this place," Henry's voice raised and echoed off the walls of the small room. "He can't have your sleutel and he can't have our friends."

Leigh nodded again.

"It's time to come up with a plan."

18

The Dream Source

HENRY AND LEIGH WALKED for what felt like several hours following the twisting and turning of the dream river before stopping to rest their sore feet.

After Captain Electro had ferried them back to the edge of Leigh's dreamscape, they set out to find their friends who had been captured by Xander in his drive to collect the three sleutels. Leigh pointed them toward the river and they only now stopped.

Henry lowered his hand absently into the iridescent river water. He watched it break and flow around his fingers before it continued downstream toward the thousands of dreamscapes below.

"Is that the dream source?" Henry asked, pointing to the top of a waterfall in the distance.

"That's it," Leigh replied.

Indeed, further up the river, a sparkling waterfall fell off a tall cliff into a large pool that fed the river they were now following. The swirl and churn of the waterfall sent iridescent mist into the air creating arching rainbows in several directions.

"What is that at the top of the waterfall?" Henry asked.

"It's the control—the dream matrix," she said. "It allows us to access these dreams. It has a slot for each of the three sleutels."

Henry noticed that his grandmother absently reached up and squeezed the third and final sleutel that hung from her neck. Henry could see the outline of the Christmas tree that topped the dream key.

Henry could see three figures standing around the dream matrix. The outline of Xander's tall, lanky frame was distinguishable among the other figures. He was standing ankle-deep in the water high above the waterfall. With his arms tucked behind his back, it appeared he was watching them and calmly waiting for their arrival.

To each side of the dream matrix, Dickie and Clement could also clearly be seen. They stood with their hands tied behind their backs and gags across their mouths.

"They don't look like they've moved," Leigh said. "Xander is waiting there—he's waiting for us."

"At least Dickie and Clement look safe and unharmed," Henry replied.

Henry stared at Dickie and thought he looked scared, but could not tell for sure at this distance.

"What are we going to do?" Henry said as he looked at his grandmother. "Is there a plan?"

His grandmother nodded, but never took her eyes off their friends standing next to Xander near the dream matrix.

"We aren't strong enough to defeat Xander and his goons," she said thoughtfully. "But that doesn't mean we can't create some confusion and hope for the best."

Henry was struck by the look on his grandmother's face. Her lips curled into a Cheshire cat grin that gave her the youthful look of a long-lost mischievous youth.

"Hopefully that confusion will give us time to free our friends and escape with the final sleutel."

Henry nodded.

Leigh quickly described to Henry what she intended to do.

"Do you think that will work?" Henry asked.

"I certainly hope so—for the sake of our friends and these dreamscapes."

Henry stood, but his grandmother rested her hand on his arm and looked intently at him.

"There are no limits in a dreamscape," she said intently. "The dreamer controls every aspect of that space. We can enter the dreams, but we can't change them."

Henry nodded. He was unsure what to do with that information.

Henry followed Leigh along the translucent river as they began their climb up the cliffs next to the waterfall. The calming sound of the steady trickle of the river was slowly replaced by the churning sound of the waterfall. Henry was not confident in the plan his grandmother had described, but he had been unable to think of anything better. After a long day of playing cat and mouse through various dreamscapes, his nerves were shot and his fears were rising.

Small pebbles tumbled down behind Leigh and Henry as the angle of the climb began to increase. Henry's legs burned and his feet ached.

As they reached the top of the cliff, Henry's stomach dropped and he could taste the fear rising in the back of his mouth. Dozens of men—Xander's goons—were standing in a semi-circle around the dream matrix. Xander stood as still as ever waiting on their arrival. Dickie and Clement were still bound on either side of the dream matrix.

Leigh nodded to Henry to let him know she was initiating their plan. Henry followed her as she stepped off into the iridescent waters just above the waterfall. The water was flowing much faster now and he could feel it pulling and tugging on his feet. He watched as his grandmother gingerly stepped closer to Xander and the dream matrix.

"What have you done, Xander?" Leigh shouted over the steady roar of the nearby falls.

"My, my," Xander replied. "Whatever you do you mean?"

"This isn't you," Leigh said, pointing toward Dickie and Clement. "You used to care about people."

Leigh took several steps toward Xander and the two hostages.

"We created the dream matrix to help preserve and protect dreams—not destroy them!" Leigh shouted.

Xander flicked his hand dismissing her suggestion like an annoying insect.

"People don't deserve to dream," Xander said as he raised his arms out and above his head. "They are silly creatures who constantly waste their opportunities and live in the anxiety of their choices."

Leigh took several steps closer to the edge of the waterfall. Henry watched as the semi-circle of Xander's goons slowly tightened around Xander and Leigh.

"You have no right to judge people," she said. "Dreams are an outlet for people to escape and have time to process their decisions."

"They should live in their choices—not escape like a coward," Xander said.

The ring of goons crept even closer as if driven by the dismissive words of their master.

"You're wrong," Leigh shouted as she edged closer to the falls. "You're better than this."

"Not anymore," Xander replied coldly. "Now give me the third sleutel –your sleutel– so I can shut down this infernal machine and end this ridiculous charade."

"I don't have it," Leigh replied.

Xander shook his head absently.

"But of course you do," Xander said. "It's hanging around your neck as it always has."

"Grab her!" Xander shouted.

Several goons stepped forward and grabbed Leigh roughly by the arms. They hauled her through the water until she stood in front of Xander. A wide grin split his face.

"You can't win," Leigh said as she struggled against the firm hold of her captures. "You'll never get all three sleutels."

Xander pulled out the other two sleutels and held them in front of Leigh's face in the shape of a V.

"Oh no?" Xander said snidely. "But this is it—my victory."

While his goons continued to hold Leigh, Xander turned and stepped toward the dream matrix. He inserted one sleutel on the left side and another on the right side which glowed red and blue in the matrix. One final slot remained open—the last sentinel protecting the thousands of dreamscapes below.

"And now for the crown jewel," Xander said, turning back toward Leigh.

Leigh gritted her teeth and continued to struggle against her captors. Xander put his hand around Leigh's head and leaned forward so that their foreheads were touching.

"You should not have fought me," Xander said quietly. "It is time for this foolishness to end."

Xander pulled hard which snatched the necklace free from Leigh's neck. He turned to his remaining goons and held the necklace high for all to see.

"To our success!" Xander shouted.

But the goons did not respond enthusiastically. Instead, they exchanged looks between each other unsure of what to do. Xander quickly looked at the necklace intertwined through his fingers and hanging from his hand.

"It's gone!" Xander shouted. "Where is the third sleutel?!"

Xander spun quickly and stormed back to Leigh kicking iridescent water in all directions.

"Where is the sleutel?" He demanded. "You would not have left it unprotected and you wouldn't have given it to just anyone."

A smile slowly curled across Leigh's face.

"You're right, dummy," Henry said. "She didn't leave it with just anyone."

Henry held the sleutel between his fingers high enough to be seen. He stood near the edge of the waterfall with Dickie and Clement standing to each side.

Xander's face burned with intensity.

"You dare to try and trick me?" Xander snarled. "I will not be stopped."

Xander ran directly at Henry knocking him off the edge and plummeting down the waterfall into the iridescent churn below.

19

Christmas Trees

HENRY'S BRAIN WAS SIMULTANEOUSLY processing the world in slow motion while quickly falling through the wall of mist the waterfall was putting off. He held on to the sleutel as tight as he could even as he and Xander plunged over the edge of the waterfall.

Henry could see the evil sneer still present on Xander's face. Above the sneer, Xander's eyes were empty and evil-looking. Henry was confident that Xander's hatred was not limited to just him, his grandmother, and their friends, but rather the entire world. In addition to the full desire to survive (from a likely fatal plunge off a large waterfall), Henry was convinced that this man could not be allowed to get the third sleutel.

When Henry and Xander hit the water their bodies separated for the first time. Henry felt like every nerve in his body was afire with the wet sting of such a high plunge. His body was thrown into a tumult getting tossed and turned in all directions. Henry was unclear which way was up and which way was down. He had the strangest sensation of feeling like a forgotten sock in a washing machine.

Just before full panic set in, Henry gulped air as his head broke through the surface. He was on the far side of a large pool with the waterfall far off in the distance. He was amazed at how far the water flow had pushed him. He could see Dickie, Clement, and his grandmother running down the hillside. Xander's goons were mostly standing at the top of the waterfall seemingly unsure of what to do. Without the presence of their master and his obsession with the sleutels, they were lost.

"The sleutel!" Leigh screamed from a distance.

Henry glanced in his hand, but the sleutel was gone. The churn of the rapids must have dislodged it. Henry frantically swung his hands side to side in the water in the desperate hope it would reappear.

"Is this what you're looking for?"

Henry glanced up and saw Xander standing on the nearby riverbank holding the final sleutel in his hand. Henry scrambled out of the water to come face-to-face with his nemesis.

"You can't do this, Xander," Henry said. "You can't crush people's dreams—you can't just turn off their dreamscapes."

Dickie, Clement, and a small group of Xander's goons had arrived and were watching Henry and Xander from the other side of the river. Xander turned and dramatically held the yellow sleutel above his head like a trophy. Xander had won.

"I now control all three sleutels," Xander yelled. "I can and will turn off the matrix and dissolve the dreamscapes."

Henry felt defeated. His grandmother's plan had failed and Xander had gotten what he wanted.

"Hold them steady while I walk back to the dream matrix," Xander directed at several goons who had recently arrived.

Henry fell to his knees in disappointment and exhaustion. Earlier today he had not even known that his grandmother was an inventor, much less had invented a way to access everyone's dream space. He had not only seen but experienced worlds of such immense imagination that he could not even begin to think about what would happen if people could not access their spaces. Hope might be lost if people's escape was impossible.

He needed a way to fix this. He could not dream of a way to prevent Xander from reuniting the sleutels and destroying these worlds forever. He closed his eyes, breathed deeply, and tried to calmly think through the options. He felt like he was fading, slowly fading, on the edge of a dream. For a moment, all Henry could see was the Christmas tree in his grandmother's snow globe and that had topped her sleutel. Then he knew exactly what he had to do.

"It's fitting that you two were here to see this," Xander said to Leigh and Clement. "We were all together to start this and now we'll all be together to end it."

"You can't do this," Clement pleaded.

"Who's gonna stop me now?" Xander laughed.

"You always forget about me, dummy," Henry said as he charged at Xander.

Henry had never really enjoyed football in school, but felt confident that Coach Benedict would have been proud of his form as he tackled Xander to the ground. Out of the corner of his eye, Henry saw the silver glint as the sleutel flew from Xander's hand. Henry quickly got up to face Xander again.

Xander got to his knees and turned again to Henry.

"You silly boy," Xander said dismissively. "You merely delayed the inevitable."

"I think you'll find that you're wrong this time," Henry said with a smile.

"Don't be ridiculous!" Xander spat. "I'm sure your grandmother's sleutel is right here."

Xander turned away from Henry to discover that he was surrounded by trees—Christmas trees—that were covered in ornaments that looked decidedly like the final sleutel.

"What have you done, boy?" Xander said as he examined the branches of the nearby trees. "There must be thousands of trees here—these all look alike!"

"It seems like I need to explain a few things," Henry said with more confidence than he felt.

"Don't patronize me, kid," Xander responded irritably.

"While you were bragging about destroying the dreamscapes, I tried to imagine how to defeat you," Henry said slowly.

Xander stared at him, not understanding. Henry stole a glance at his grandmother who seemed to slowly be understanding what was going on. Dickie and Clement still looked on with shock.

"So I took a nap and dreamed," Henry replied with a flourish. "You're now in my dreamscape, which as you already noted is simply filled with trees. Thousands upon thousands of matching, decorated trees."

Xander's nostrils flared and his face began to redden. "Where is the sleutel?!"

"Oh, it's here," Henry said. "I'm sure you can find it."

"Tell me where it is!" Xander bellowed.

Henry waded across the river ignoring Xander's question. He slowly approached the spot where Dickie, Clement, and his grandmother were being held. He looked at the goons one by one realizing they were again confused.

"You guys should really help your boss," Henry said to the goons. "He's gonna need it."

The goons exchanged a look before releasing their hostages and wading across the river to help their boss.

Henry, Dickie, Clement, and Leigh hugged.

Henry looked back at Xander who was crawling on hands and knees from tree to tree comparing one key to the next. For a moment, Henry felt a pang of guilt but then remembered what Xander had put them through.

"Let's get out of here," Henry said as he turned and walked away.

20

The Mist

"So you trapped Xander in your dreamscape?" Dickie asked. "Like you just dropped it right over him?"

"That pretty much sums it up," Henry said with a smile. "It wasn't the plan we drew up, but in the end, it worked."

"How did you know it would work?" Leigh asked with the grin of a proud grandmother.

"It was your reminder," Henry replied to her. "You reminded me that dreamers controlled the dream. I calmed myself down and fell asleep, but just before that I had a vision of your Christmas tree and realized that the only thing that would stop Xander was more sleutels."

The four of them returned to silence much like earlier when they had left Xander and his goons searching through the field of sleutel-filled Christmas trees. They had followed the river back down into the dreamscapes reversing the path Henry and Leigh had taken earlier.

They had rarely spoken as they walked.

Eventually, they made it back to the Station of Dreams and now sat on a bench under a large mechanical clock near where they had all arrived earlier. The light purple smoke had long dissipated and the dream train was gone. The station was empty and it was quiet.

"I've been thinking," Dickie said, leaning forward and looking at Henry. "What will happen once Xander finds the third sleutel? Won't he just deactivate the dream matrix?"

"I made that a rule of my dreamscape," Henry said. "Xander is never allowed to leave."

"That's brilliant," Dickie said impressively.

Henry grinned, basking in his friend's acknowledgment.

"But more importantly," Leigh said. "Henry still has the sleutel."

Henry nodded. He had felt the weight of his grandmother's sleutel in his pocket for the entire walk back to the station. He had wanted to pull it out, look at it, and make sure it really was the third sleutel. He was afraid Clement would somehow see it, understand the deception, and stop searching through the trees.

Henry pulled the sleutel from his pocket and looked at it as it sat in the palm of his hand. He slowly pushed it out toward his grandmother.

"I think this is yours," Henry said to Leigh.

Leigh closed Henry's hand around the sleutel.

"I think you've shown that you can protect it," Leigh said quietly. "I'd like you to keep it and protect it."

Henry was speechless. The adventure they all just experienced was something he would never forget. Having this new responsibility was unimaginable even in a land overflowing with imagination. Henry returned the sleutel to his pocket and sat down on the bench.

After a few moments, Dickie stood and faced the others.

"This has been great—like really great," Dickie said. "But how do we get home—how do we stop dreaming?"

"Can't we just take the train back?" Henry said.

Clement and Leigh exchanged a look of mutual understanding.

"You can't take the train back," Clement said. "That's not how it works."

"Why not?" Henry asked.

"Have you ever had the sensation of falling when you sleep?" Clement asked.

"Sure," Dickie said. "All the time."

"And what happens when you fall in the dream?" Leigh asked, continuing the line of questions.

"I wake up?" Dickie said. "I wake up!"

Dickie stepped up on the platform and fell back landing hard on the dream station surface.

"It didn't work," Dickie said, standing up and rubbing the back of his head. "I fell but I'm still here."

Clement and Leigh laughed together. The sound was pleasant in the otherwise quiet calm.

"Follow us," Leigh said, standing and walking away.

As directed, Henry and Dickie followed Clement and Leigh as they walked down a path away from the train station. In the distance, Henry could see what appeared to be a cliff that was shrouded in mist not too far down the path.

"Is that where we are headed?" Henry asked, pointing at the wall of mist.

Clement nodded.

A few moments later, Henry and Clement stopped in front of a tall pole with a sign that said "Dream Zipper."

"What's a dream zipper?" Dickie asked.

"This is how we go home," Leigh said with a smile. "This is a zip line—a dream zipper."

"But you can't see where it goes," Henry said. "It just runs out into the mist."

"Good observation, my boy," Clement said. "The end of a dream is often blurred. Even though we've found a way to visit this land and move in and out of dreams, we have to move through that blur to leave."

A thick rope traveled from the sign out into the mist. Henry glanced at Dickie who looked less than convinced.

"We know you boys have been through a lot," Leigh said. "But trust us that this is safe and will get you home."

Henry and Dickie exchanged looks and nodded.

"We've seen just about everything today," Henry said, "Why not take a dream zipper to end it?"

The four of them exchanged a laugh.

"I'll head back first," Leigh said. "I will be there when you get back."

Leigh grabbed a silver bar hanging from the line.

"Just step off and when you're ready, let go," Leigh said.

"Just let go?" Dickie's voice pitched up.

Clement squeezed Dickie's shoulder and smiled.

Leigh held the bar and stepped out. Henry watched as the mist opened and then wrapped around her like a hug of a long-lost friend. He anxiously stared at the mist half expecting to hear panicked screams or for her to be magically rejected back into the dream space. But neither happened and Henry slowly felt a sense of relief and pending closure to their long adventure.

"You're up next, Dickie," Clement said with a smile.

Dickie wrapped his hands around the handle of the bar which had reappeared.

"See you on the other side?" Dickie asked.

"See you on the other side," Henry answered.

Dickie took a deep breath and stepped off into the mist. Yet again the mist opened and then closed behind obscuring Dickie from view.

Henry stepped forward to assume the position, but a new thought occurred to him.

"Where do you land at the end of the dream zipper?" Henry asked Clement.

"You will wake up wherever you started the dream," Clement said. "You, Dickie, and your grandmother will all appear back at her house where you accessed the dream space."

"So you'll end up back at your house?" Henry asked.

Henry noticed Clement's expression changed. The joyous smile he had carried since they left Xander had faded into a mixture of sadness, acceptance, and resolve.

"I'm not going back, Henry."

"What do you mean?"

I'm going to stay in dreamland—go back to Reverseland," Clement replied. "The world here is more interesting than anything I have waiting for me back home. Not to mention that somebody probably needs to keep an eye on Xander."

"Does my grandmother know?" Henry asked.

"Yes," Clement said quietly. "I told her earlier and she understood."

Henry looked at the man again. He wanted to go home more than anything he could think of, but part of him understood. Dreamland was filled with depths of imagination beyond compare. As long as the sleutels were protected and Xander was secured, people's dreams would continue to be protected.

"Thank you, Henry," Clement said as he extended his hand. "For everything you've done here."

Henry took the man's hand and shook it vigorously.

Three loud clangs echoed off the walls of the valley as the clock at the Station of Dreams announced some unknown time. Henry looked back up the path they walked.

"Now it's time to go," Clement said quickly. "They are probably wondering where you are."

As he had witnessed twice before, Henry slid his fingers over the reappeared bar and stepped forward. He could hear the thumping of his heart in his ears. He nodded at Clement one more time before stepping forward into the mist. He saw it separate for him and then wrap itself back around him in a cool embrace plunging him into a pool of gray.

21

Out in the Garden

THE WALLS OF GRAY carried off in every direction as Henry was engulfed by the mist. Henry could feel the coolness of the mist rush across his face as his full weight hung from the bar. He strained his eyes to look ahead assuming he would see his grandmother's house or some other signal to show the end of the dream zipper. But all he could see was the sea of gray.

He was unsure how long he would be able to hold on as his arms began to burn from the dangle of his weight. He closed his eyes tight, wishing himself to wake. All he could focus on was his ever-weakening grip. His hope of finding the landing spot faded as fast as his strength.

With growing panic, Henry could feel several fingers slip from his grip on the bar. To his utter fear, the cool air of the mist seemed to be tickling and tugging at his remaining fingers. He was not going to make it.

Henry let out a loud cry as his remaining fingers finally slipped from the bar and he fell spinning, turning, and twisting through the white mist . . . until he wasn't.

The world went dark around Henry. He saw spots in his vision as his eyes adjusted to the quick change from the brightness of the mist to the darkness around him now.

"Henry?" A familiar voice said. "Your vision will adjust in a moment."

The voice was right. Henry could start to see the outline of lines and shapes.

"I think he's coming around," another voice said.

Henry sat up and continued to blink heavily. He could see the two figures standing on each side of him.

"Grandma?" Henry asked. "Dickie?"

The two figures gave a quick shout of joy. The smaller of the two kneeled next to Henry.

"It's a pretty wild ride, huh?" Dickie said, smiling. "Welcome back."

Dickie grabbed Henry's arm and helped him stand up. Henry could now see the outline of his grandmother's secret room. The eerie blue light bathed the workbenches and square table in the middle of the room.

"How are you feeling?" Leigh asked as she looked intently into his eyes. "Sometimes the dream zipper can be pretty disorienting."

"I'm okay," Henry said quickly.

"Let's get out of this tiny, dark room," Leigh said. "My feet are aching and my back is calling for a rest in my chair."

Leigh walked toward the door that Henry and Dickie had found earlier.

"Wait!" Dickie shouted.

Leigh turned, confused by Dickie's direction.

"Before we found this room," Dickie said, "We found your house was in shambles where Xander's men had tossed everything about looking for the sleutel."

"Good thing they didn't find it," Leigh said, turning back toward the door.

"Wait," Henry said, understanding what Dickie was getting at. "Mom had called the police since you were missing. They are probably just on the other side of that door."

Leigh nodded twice acknowledging Henry's and Dickie's concern.

"We'll just have to use the back door."

"The back door?" Dickie asked. "You have a backdoor to a secret room?"

"But of course," Leigh said playfully. "Follow me."

Leigh walked to the far side of the room and began methodically pulling and pushing various unseen levers. With a soft hiss and a sliver of light, a narrow door appeared. Henry could see his grandmother's garden in the distance. Henry and Dickie followed Leigh out the door which quickly closed behind them. Henry was disoriented again as the brightness of the sunlight hurt his eyes.

"Grandma?" Henry asked. "How long were we in dreamland?"

"Not long." She replied quickly. "Time is a funny thing and runs very differently in dreams."

"How do we explain all this to the police?" Dickie asked.

"Just follow my lead," Leigh said as she winked at the boys.

Leigh walked over to a small table that held two small potted plants and several gardening instruments. Henry watched as Leigh reached into one of the small pots and pinched a small amount of dirt which she promptly rubbed on her forehead and cheeks. She pulled on a pair of blue gardening gloves and began to walk toward the front of the house. The boys moved quickly to keep up.

As they rounded the corner of the house, Henry could see his mother talking to the police officer.

"I'm worried about her, Officer." Henry's mother said. "She's never just disappeared before. At her age and health, she would likely get hurt if she wandered off."

"How old do you think I am?" Leigh asked as she walked straight toward the police officer.

The thin police officer exchanged looks between the two women. He tugged at his belt causing his keys and tools to jingle.

"Where were you, Mom?" Henry's mother asked Leigh.

"I was in my garden doing some pruning," she said, showing her recently gloved hands. "Henry and his friend found me and told me you had arrived."

Henry's mother glanced at the boys. For a moment, Henry was convinced she would somehow read their minds or force them to reveal where they had been.

"Is that right, boys?" She asked aggressively.

Dickie and Henry nodded.

"Someone broke into your house." Henry's mother said, returning her attention to Leigh.

"Oh dear," Leigh said.

"Did you hear or see anything, ma'am?" The police officer asked. "Do you know if anything of value was taken?"

"Oh, I doubt it," Leigh said with a hidden wink for Henry. "I'm sorry my daughter bothered you today."

"But, Mom, your house is a mess," Henry's mother said. "Don't you want to look around?"

"Oh, we'll look around eventually," Leigh replied. "But let's let this fine officer go on to more serious matters."

Henry's mom was perplexed. The officer seemed amused.

"If you do find anything missing, please let us know," the officer replied, walking back to his car.

"Let's go inside and have a look," Henry's Mom said.

"Not just yet," Leigh replied, looking at Henry. "I think we should go visit Grandpa at the care facility first—he's been on my mind recently."

"Sounds great," Henry replied with a smile.